THREE BEARS

Short Mysteries from PI Bear Jacobs

Linda B. Myers

About This Book

Three Bears is a work of fiction. Names, characters, places and happenings are from the author's imagination. Any resemblance to actual persons - living or dead - events or locales is entirely coincidental.

Published 2019 by Mycomm One
ISBN: 978-0-9986747-9-7
Cover design: www.introstudio.me
Interior design: Heidi Hansen
For updates and chatter:
www.LindaBMyers.com
Facebook.com/lindabmyers.author
myerslindab@gmail.com

DEDICATION

For my sister, Donna Whichello.

Bear wouldn't have a clue without her help.

CONTENTS

BEAR AND THE BURRITO

BEAR AND THE BURRITO

CHAPTER ONE

Case Notes
June 4, 2 a.m.

In those darkest hours before dawn, the ones when a nightmare leaves you disturbed for the rest of the day, the howl began. It was a cry of madness, forlorn and long and fundamental.

I fought the bed covers to sit up straight as Eunice snapped on the light. She cried, "What on earth?"

"Not sure it is on earth," I answered, grabbing my robe first and my walker next. Not wearing my prosthetic leg at night I needed the walker. I worked my way to our door and ventured into the dark hall.

Through the blackness, I saw a form and heard it breathe. It was big and hunched, totally still, as though listening in the dark.

"Morning, Lily," it said.

"Bear! What the hell are you doing out here in the dark?"

"Same as you, I imagine. Tracking down that caterwauling."

1

"I know you're the big shot detective and all, but could we do it in the light?" I turned on the overheads that lit up the hall.

"Sure, turn on the light if you can't use your ears in the dark. Quite a handicap, I'd say, for a PI's assistant."

Not sure if I've mentioned lately that Bear Jacobs is an evil-tempered crab of a shamus when he's in a really good mood, much less when something has lured him out of his den in the night.

"BEWHEAWHEAWHEAH."

There it was again. Not a ghoul exactly, nor a coyote howl, nor ululating women. Not Baby Benny adding his two cents.

"Is it badly tuned strings?" asked Eunice, hands over her ears. She'd joined us but only after applying a bit of blush.

"I think it's an ass," I said.

"Around here, it must be a horse's ass." Bear was referring to the fact that Latin's Ranch Adult Family Care is the home of champion Paso Finos as well as a smattering of other horses owned by boarders. Jessica Winslow cares for four-leggers as well as two-leggers like us. Well, some of us have two legs. As I've mentioned, I have one.

"We'll see what's going on," said Jessica, hurrying down the stairs as she tied her bathrobe sash. "You guys stay here."

Her husband, Ben, came behind her, yawning as he plopped Baby Benny into Bear's obliging grasp.

Jess didn't really think we'd gather in the living room to await a field report. She knows better than that. We headed out back, and I unplugged our golf cart, Sitting Bull. Eunice, Baby Benny, Bear, and I loaded up to head for the barn, following Jessica and Ben who had swapped Baby Benny for a baseball bat.

That's how the case of Bear and the Burrito began.

Lily Gilbert, Night-stalking Assistant to PI Bear Jacobs

Bear cruised to a quiet stop inside the barn. He stepped out of the golf cart, grabbed his quad cane from Eunice who was sitting in the back, then took Benny from Lily's arms; she needed both hands to manage her walker. Bear tucked the little guy into the crook of his elbow and maneuvered the cane with his other hand.

Jessica, Ben, and their barn manager, Sam Hart, were all in their night clothes, staring into the stall of the ancient workhorse, Gina Lola. Bear felt a chill for the old gray mare, but she looked through the open top of her Dutch door, her ears pricked forward as she watched them approach. She seemed fine as she nickered a greeting to the latecomers.

Besides, Jessica, Ben and Sam weren't staring at her. They were eyeballing the area of the stall hidden by the lower half of her gate. Bear, Lily and Eunice crushed forward to take a peek inside.

"BEWHEAWHEAWHEAH."

A pinto burro stood in the straw next to Gina Lola. Not a full-sized burro. A miniature donkey, tiny and adorable, with the voice of a banshee.

"BEWHEAWHEAWHEAH," it brayed again. Everyone leaned back as if blown away by an air raid siren. Eunice cupped hands over her ears, and so did Jessica. But not Baby Benny. Bear felt the baby squirm, fill his little lungs, and burst out an answer. "WAWAGUBANU?"

The donkey put its nose up, up to the top of the half door, reaching as high as it could.

Baby Benny gurgled and reached out a fat little hand. The miniature burro nickered.

"Appear to be kindred spirits," Bear said.

"You mean that both are adorable, right? Not too noisy, right?" Jessica turned, squinting a warning at Bear. Nobody criticized her baby.

"Sure that's what I mean. Adorable. Both of them." Bear rolled his eyes. "Baby Benny and a little burro. Who's got a camera?"

"Little burro. *Burrito*," said Lily making air quotes with her fingers. "A name is born."

"But who does it belong to?"

"Where did it come from?"

"Why is it here?"

"Does it need milk?"

"It's a grown up, isn't it?"

"Who put it in with Gina Lola?"

"Is it a colt or a filly?"

"Burros are Jacks and Jennys, I think."

"BEWHEAWHEAWHEAH."

As Bear listened, he realized not only a name but another mystery was born. It was about damn time. Everyone at Latin's Ranch needed something to divert them from the hole left that spring by Alita and Rick, the two aides who had not returned with them from the cruise to Alaska. Jessica was trying hard to replace them, but it was never easy to find candidates who met her standards. Or the standards of their senior aide, Chrissie, for that matter.

* * *

The morning was a sunbathed beauty, Washington's reward for putting up with a winter of rain. The Latin's Ranch residents were sitting on the back patio, sharing mugs of

4

steaming coffee and hot conchas. Their cook Aurora made the sweet rolls with a top layer of strawberry or chocolate. Jessica had called her friend, Deputy Sheriff Josephine Keegan, to let her know some weird game was afoot. "Well, maybe the game is ahoof," she corrected.

She also left a message for Doc McGrath to come examine the mini-donkey. "At least that's what I think it is," she'd said into her cell phone between bites of the sweet bun.

Now they were waiting for the doc to arrive. Bear hefted his mighty self out of the patio chair, announcing, "Guess I'll go around front to meet him. Bring him back here before he goes up to the barn. You know, the place where most people keep their livestock."

He *kachunked* on his quad cane through the house and out to the front porch to await the veterinarian. Latin's Ranch's new pup, a gift from the resident mobster, Frankie, joined him. Bear began throwing the battered tennis ball that the pup adored. The Alaskan husky, named Good Fella, could binge-run like all his sled dog ancestors. "I think I'm developing a pitching arm," Bear said to the pooch, whizzing the ball over a patch of new Japanese maples all the way to the tree line of the woods. The pup got there before the ball did and caught it on the fly.

A middle-aged van growled its way to a stop in the driveway. Doc McGrath dismounted. "Not going to the barn?" The vet raised a questioning eyebrow as Bear *kachunked* to the van.

"Nope. The back yard." Bear threw the soggy ball again then headed around the house.

"Gimme a minute," Doc said.

Bear stopped, turned, and watched the vet circle to the back of his van, heard him open the back door, then slam it closed.

"Why the back yard?" As the vet circled back to the front of the van, Bear saw he was carrying another tiny burro in his arms. He set it down, and as it wobbled a moment on knobby-kneed legs, he attached a lead to its halter.

Hmm, Bear thought. *Sometimes you get the answer before you ask the question.* There was a clue here that the veterinarian had been the late night donkey delivery man. But Bear merely said, "Mystery Beast Number One is paying a visit to Baby Benny."

Good Fella yipped in delight to announce Doc McGrath to the other Latin's Ranch residents in the backyard. Since he had the ball in his mouth his woofs were muffled, but his leaps and twists made his joy over a new arrival abundantly clear. The vet smiled, laugh lines deepening around his eyes. "Hope Jessica knows she's not raising much of a guard dog here."

Bear wondered if Doc was starting to squint, like a lot of forty-somethings tend to do. Eye glasses were probably just around the corner.

Lily, Eunice, Charlie, and Jessica were seated on the patio when the men came into sight. Eunice saw them first, looking up from the razzle-dazzle she was stitching to a length of spandex. "Will you look at that!"

Lily put down the crossword puzzle, and Jessica stared. She stood, demanding, "Do you know you're leading another burro?"

"Figured you might have room for another little critter," the vet said.

The first burro was curled on the lawn next to Baby Benny who had mastered the art of sitting upright. He was happily twisting a burro ear toward his mouth. The burro nuzzled the baby, pushing him over with his nose. Like a bozo doll, Benny righted himself with a squawk and began the ear game all over again.

Meanwhile, Jo Keegan supervised the play. Bending over to be sure that the little fist was not too tight, she said, "It's against protocol to grab a suspect by the ears, Benny." She kissed the top of his head. Her backside, never at its best in her sheriff uniform, still looked okey dokey to at least one party.

"My, oh my, that's a fine-looking ass," Doc mumbled to himself.

Bear overheard. "You're here to examine the four-legger, Doc, not the two-legger."

Doc grinned, then approached the threesome on the grass. He released the burro on the lead, and it circled then lay down beside the other.

After the two little beasts greeted each other like friends, snuffling and nipping and braying, the vet said, "Hi. I'm Doc."

The deputy straightened. "I'm Jo. Jessica's friend."

As the two shook hands, Jessica said, "Sorry, I figured you probably knew each other. Jo is a friend, sure, but also a deputy sheriff. I asked her to stop by. Didn't want anyone thinking I'm rustling livestock."

Her two visitors appeared to ignore her.

Deputy Sheriff Josephine Keegan of the Major Crimes Unit smiled at Doc.

Doctor of Veterinary Medicine Bohannan McGrath smiled at Jo.

Even Bear, who was usually oblivious to such things, felt the chemical reaction. Invisible test tubes fizzed, flasks smoked, pipettes piped, and molecules definitely rearranged.

"Um, Doc?" Jessica asked as she swept up Baby Benny to move him out of the way. "The donkeys are down here. Explain yourself."

* * *

"Yes, I left the burro here last night," the vet said, sipping a cup of coffee and tasting a concha. "Emmm. Heaven."

"Concha. A pretty good name for that second little cutie," observed Eunice.

Lily nodded. "Concha it is. Burrito and Concha."

Bear huffed at the cuteness overload.

Jessica asked Doc, "Why didn't you knock last night?"

"Didn't want to wake you. Guess that plan failed."

"I'll say. Burrito had a strong opinion about it," Charlie said.

"Oh, Charlie, you never even heard him over your own snoring," Lily said.

"Did, too. Just wanted to stay out of the way."

The vet swallowed another bite then said, "I had to leave him, Jess, and I figured your old work horse would be an obliging donkey-sitter. Couldn't get both burros at the same time. So I dropped him off then went back for her."

"But why..."

"Jess, the little guy's healthy still, but severely underweight. Starving. He couldn't stay where he was."

"You mean his owner wasn't feeding him?" Jessica's eyes popped wide in surprise then narrowed in anger. Her cheeks went from pink to fire engine red in under sixty seconds.

Bear had seen that flash of anger occasionally for some damn thing he'd done. It was scary...kind of like she needed an exorcist. At least it was short-lived.

The vet looked sheepish as he pleaded, "You have room for him? I'll pay his keep."

"Not angry with you, Doc. And he'd damn near fit in a shoe box. 'Course I have room. What kind of owner wouldn't feed a sweetheart like him? And you're right. Gina Lola likes him just fine." Jessica's head of steam dissipated.

"Concha, too?"

Jessica stopped for a moment. "Well, sure, I guess so. But where are they from? Who owns them?"

"Not sure you want to know, so I'm not saying. At least not in front of the law." He beamed at the deputy. "That okay with you, Deputy? Don't need to place them with Donkey Protective Services?"

She laughed at his joke a little too much. "I'm sure Latin's Ranch is donkey heaven."

At that minute she received a call on her radio. She sighed, then stood to take her leave. "If all is good here, I'll be on my way before I hear another word of this story." With a parting sunburst smile at the vet, she added, "Wouldn't want to arrest anyone."

This time, Doc laughed at *her* joke a little too much. He watched her go.

"Ahem," Bear grumbled. He felt a jab of concern for the cop he called Cupcake. She'd been let down badly by the last man who seemed like such a good guy. Not that it was any of his business. Not that that would stop him from butting in.

Doc appeared to remember his reason to be there. "Let Burrito and Concha eat as much hay as they want for a while, then slowly cut back. Grass will do. Donkeys get fat easier than horses."

"So they're not just ponies with long ears?" Jessica asked.

"No, ma'am. Their kind is used to hardscrabble desert fare. Far more efficient food processors than horses. It wouldn't take all that much to keep them up and running. That's why this is such a shame."

"Well, I'll fatten them up before the owner comes forward. Where's their mama?"

"Dead."

The Latin's Ranch residents reacted with a group shudder. They were all old, physically uncertain, and dependent on others. It was damn easy to empathize with the burros.

"Oh!"

"No!"

"Poor babies!"

Bear took matters in hand. The private investigator in him knew how to interrogate a witness. "Doc," he said. "You better begin again. Why are you stealing animals?"

"Me? *Stealing*?"

"You. Stealing."

Doc shrugged. "Well, maybe a little background first. Donkeys aren't at the top of the farmer food chain. The price of corn has skyrocketed ever since ethanol became a thing. Even for their cattle, some farmers are adding crumbled cookies, Skittles, cocoa powder to the feed as a cheaper supplement. The sugar replaces what's lost by less corn."

"That's not bad for cows? Or people drinking milk? Eating beef?"

Doc shrugged. "They say not. Now as to stealing..."

* * *

As Keegan circled to the front of the house and walked to her car, she noticed another visitor had arrived. The middle-aged Beetle in the driveway was pock-marked, wrinkled like an orange skin.

Maybe rolled in a gravel yard. Or a moving target on a golf range. Large hail? An asteroid shower? Keegan looked from the battered bug to the porch and saw a large man standing there. He finger-combed his hair, tucked in his shirt tail, rang the bell. Since he also discharged a wad of gum, a stream of chaw, or a gob of spit into the bushes, she assumed he hadn't noticed her observing him.

With Jessica around to the back of the house, Keegan figured she'd better ask this guy who he was. But at that moment, Will opened the front door. After a brief exchange, he invited the guy inside.

Keegan recognized Will Haverstock as a person of interest in one of Bear's past cases. Since then, he'd become Chrissie's boyfriend. Will helped fill in as an aide from time to time. *All must be well*, Keegan thought, and she went on her way.

As she got in her cruiser, her thoughts turned back to the pleasant topic of Doc McGrath. Why hadn't their paths crossed before? She might have to interrogate Jessica about the guy. Maybe she should get a pet that would need a check-up fairly often. Maybe this was one of those magical vets who could talk to the animals. He certainly sent out messages to her.

Keegan pulled out of the driveway, unaware she was whistling the happy tune from Dr. Doolittle.

CHAPTER TWO

Case Notes
June 4, 9 p.m.

Mercy, what a day. I feel as leveled as the patient in an Operation board game. Sleep will likely pass me by, though. Oh for those salad days of youth when shuteye was so simple.

The day started at two in the morning with the burro's raucous cries. And the vet's story after he arrived? Well, it was enough to make us all cry. Animal abuse. Hard to fathom. Although why would people treat animals any better than we treat each other? We can be real piles of crap.

Anyhoo, Doc talked about the plight of farm animals. Cruel owners, unknowledgeable owners, owners hit so brutally by hard times that they couldn't feed their families much less their livestock. Some of them were trodden too far down to have the slightest idea what to do next. Meanwhile, the animals went untended and unfed.

Doc said he'd suggested solutions to those who would listen; many rescue services can lend a hand or help place animals if the owners research where to turn. But that had no impact on those whose pride or mean-spiritedness stood in the way of right thinking.

"Stinkin' thinkin' is what it is," Doc said, shaking his head. "When I can, I vaccinate or medicate without payment, if the

hardliners don't see me do it. Heaven forbid they'd take charity, you know. Mostly I'm Dr. Doom to these guys, sticking my nose in their business. There's not many of them so unreasonable...but even one is one too many."

He talked while we sat in the sun, feeling safe in the care of Latin's Ranch. Animals in desperate straights aren't so different from us before this place took us in. It's not always safe to depend on the kindness of others.

"Mostly, I don't care about the reason. Just the consequence for the livestock. And that's why I'm stealing a few animals, Bear. To save the ones that would surely die. I'm hiding them in places where they're not likely to be found."

"You mean you've stashed some in other places?" Jessica asked. I could almost see the address book in her head, flipping through pages of possible respites.

"That's a question I won't answer directly, Jess," Doc said. "If anyone gets in any trouble for this, it should be me. But it seems unreasonable to expect one place to take them all."

"You just gonna keep doing it until you're caught one night?" Bear asked. I could hear him preparing the Bear lecture. But Doc cut it short.

"No more questions. You shouldn't know any more than you already do. Nobody is to blame but me."

Silly Doc. As if he could drop a bomb like this and not expect us to rally 'round. Saving domestic animals. Saving Doc. What better way for a bunch of old survivors to spend our spare time?

All afternoon, we plotted and planned.

Lily Gilbert, Activist Assistant to PI Bear Jacobs

Lily knew the staff was tired, at least what remained of the staff, following Alita's murder and Rick's disappearance into the Alaskan wilds. Jessica brought in temp aides from a nursing agency, but Chrissie was so demanding, two of them refused to return after the first week.

Tonight, Chrissie cleansed and wrapped Lily's leg. This was a job she excelled at, one of the reasons the two were closely bonded. Lily was prone to infections which could easily lead to the loss of her remaining leg. Chrissie stood in the path of such a calamity, holding the possibility at bay.

"They hired another aide today," Chrissie said as she wrapped a strip of flannel smoothly over the gauze.

"Oh, good," Lily said. "Maybe you can quit working yourself to a frazzle."

"He starts tomorrow which is just in the nick of time. Will has another commitment and can't cover the shift."

"It's been a blessing having Will with us as much as he has been." Lily was fond of him ever since the time he helped save her life. Bear's, too. And, of course, because he loved Chrissie who was not always all that lovable. Like now.

As she finished the wrap job, Chrissie frowned at the current temp who seemed terrified of touching an old woman.

"For heaven's sake, Vickie. She won't break. Hold Eunice steady while she removes her robe. Then get a glass of water for her nightstand. And put her bracelets in that box."

"She's right, dear. I won't break," Eunice said gently to the hapless Vickie. "Maybe you could tuck my slippers just here...no not back in the closet...here next to the bed where I can find them in the night."

After Chrissie and Vickie left their room, Eunice exhaled a deeply dramatic sigh.

Lily said, "I agree."

"Well, I'm sure Jessica will have it right as rain soon."

Then they were quiet. Lily was reading one of the romances she loved. She thought that maybe in her long life, she should have experimented with a Highland laird or two. Opportunity missed.

Both old women were light sleepers who drifted in and out through the night. Lily believed they never really got tired enough most days to sleep through the nights. Neither lived the exhaustive life of young women these days. Poor Chrissie. Poor Jessica.

In her younger years, Lily had plenty to keep her going, too. A war widow with a baby to raise on her own. She'd held plenty of jobs: picture framer, florist, dental lab assistant, card dealer. She kept on the move, leaving lovers and lifestyles behind, until she made it to the West Coast. Washington took, and she developed roots. Her daughter Sylvia grew and married. Lily became a master gardener. Diabetes claimed a leg and her health. She met Jessica, a grieving widow, who helped with her care. And together, they supported Sylvia with her grief when her husband died.

Lily, still sleepless, rolled to her side. Maybe it was this thing about needy animals that was making her recall bad times. After her leg was amputated, the harrowing months at Soundside Rehabilitation and Health Care had nearly flattened her. The Fun House, she called it, a nursing home filled with terrors. Grief had enclosed her like a shrink-wrap shroud. And yet, following a near miss with death, that terrifying place led her to a new life. Bear, Eunice, Charlie and she found each other there. They survived it, as did Jessica and Sylvia. Latin's Ranch was the lovechild of them all.

Frankie came along later but he was the icing on the cake, beloved most especially by Eunice, his little dove. And of course, the sad story of Baby Benny had such a happy upturn when he was adopted by his granddad Ben, and Ben's new wife, Jessica.

Would the baby suffer fetal alcohol syndrome or the results of a birth mother on unknown amounts of drugs? If so, that was a horror show yet to come. In the meantime, Baby Benny was a source of delight for everyone at Latin's Ranch. He had more grannies and gramps than a child could hope for.

Lily smiled to herself. Life goes on in surprising ways if you just let yourself go with the flow. At the moment, life seemed a safe bubble bouncing along its merry way. Just as she was about to drift off, she startled herself back to wakefulness.

Bubbles can pop.

* * *

The Latin's Ranch living room was a large, sunny space often serenaded by the two caged canaries, themselves transplants from Soundside. The room was as homey as most private residences except it appeared to have a dance floor in the middle. A wide open space accommodated the wheelchairs, walkers, and wobbly people with balance issues. Comfy furniture gathered at one end of the room, and a game table at the other was next to the archway which led to the dining room. An unfinished jigsaw was in the center of the table, started a week ago by Charlie who saw no reason to hurry through one.

Before lunch, the residents gathered at the table, their mobility equipment parked higgeldy piggeldy around the edges. Jessica joined them, by their request.

"What's up, gang?" she asked. She held the fat little personage of Baby Benny on her lap.

Lily wasted none of the caregiver's time and began, "We'd like to help Doc."

"I would, too, Lily, you know that. We'll take the..."

"But what's happening is illegal, and you don't want Latin's Ranch in trouble."

"Well, true. There is that." She untangled a baby fist from one of her curls. Baby Benny let out a blat of irritation.

Lily allowed him to grab her finger as a consolation prize. Then she continued to plead her case. "We don't want that, either, Jessica. Anything that endangers Latin's Ranch endangers us."

"Here, here," agreed Eunice and Charlie, together.

Frankie cut in with a low murmur. "I can deal with these people who hurt the donkeys, but my little dove tells me no."

Lily saw relief flash through the caregiver's eyes that the mob would not be set loose on the local farm population. Jessica said, "Ah, no. Not sure the solution should have such a permanent impact on the community."

"Nonetheless," Lily went on, "we want to help. But we'd like you to stay out of it. In order to protect you."

Eunice loved the words of crime. "We'll run the con. Commit the caper. Pull the fast one."

Bear groaned.

"Double deal the dumb clucks."

Bear growled.

"Okay, I'm done," Eunice said.

"Our idea is a Latin's *Farm* housed within Latin's Ranch," Lily said, ignoring the interruption.

Jessica said, "That's silly. I'll know the animals are here. I'll *see* them for heaven's sake."

"Yes, but Doc gives the critters to us, not to you. Of course you'll know they're here, but not how we got them. As far as you know they're just our pets."

"And we'll pay for feed. I have great plans for selling Latin's Ranch crafts. Everyone's in. Well, Bear is still thinking about it." Eunice shot him a stink eye that could have seared the eyebrows off his grizzled head.

"But where will we keep them?" Jessica asked. "The barn's pretty full."

Charlie blurted, "Sam says he doesn't mind the burros, so a llama, maybe a goat wouldn't be all that much more, would it? A piglet, maybe?"

"So you've talked to Sam already."

Lily confessed. "Yes. Sam said he'd build a couple extra stalls out in the shed. But only with your okay, of course. Sam was very definite about that."

Eunice enthused, "We can lead the beasties to the pastures and back to the stalls and shower them with affection. Doc can find us an assistant to clean stalls and groom if we need help; he has animal-crazy kids ask for jobs all the time."

"So you've talked to Doc already, too."

"Well, yes." Lily confessed again.

19

Bear weighed in. "Jessica, these nut jobs think it would be good for us, a project we could share to keep us away from more dangerous pursuits."

That did the trick. Keeping a lid on Bear's investigations was always a concern for Jessica. She caved. "Okay, okay. Let me think about how best to..."

At that moment, two things happened. Benny produced another blat, this time from the opposite end of the baby. It was deadly as it permeated the room. Simultaneously, the cook, Aurora, entered the room to say, "The new aide came to the back door. He's here."

The gang looked up. Eunice gasped. As the color drained from her face, she cried, "Oh my god. It's Arnie."

A beat later, the identity came to Bear. He yelled, "Vinny, get in here." The bodyguard was never far from Frankie.

Vinny appeared in an instant, silent as a ghost, muscled and threatening as a jungle cat.

Bear said, "Escort this asshole off the premises."

Vinny cut his eyes over to Frankie.

Frankie looked surprised but nodded just once. "As Signore Bear wishes."

Vinny approached Arnie who raised his hands and pleaded, "Wait, now wait. What the fuck? Get back..."

Vinny grabbed one arm, swung the younger man around, and marched him out the front door in a headlock, murmuring, "You will accompany Vinny with no questions. You will not return."

Bear *kachunked* to the wide open door. He felt the others gather around him as he pulled out his phone. When the man looked back at them, as if hoping for help, Bear took his picture. "Fat chance of help from us," Bear mumbled to his gang. Together, they watched Vinny escort Arnie to a battered orange Beetle and stand guard until the bug headed up the driveway and away.

It all happened in a blink. Then Jessica found her voice and demanded, "Bear! What on earth was that all about?"

"Might be Baby Benny smelling like a dirty diaper, Jessica. But I'm thinking it was that piece of shit, as well."

CHAPTER THREE

Case Notes
June 5, 3 p.m.

It took a while for Eunice to calm down, Bear to drain his anger, Vinny to appear less murderous, and Jessica to change the baby's diaper then deliver him to his crib. Guess Charlie and I were het up, too. If we'd been horses, Sam Hart would have walked us around to cool off following such a workout.

As humans, we required the restorative power of tea. After cups were served by a highly concerned Chrissie, we explained to each other what the hell had happened.

Will Haverstock didn't know Arnie Burgess. So when he brought him in for an interview and deposited him in Jessica's office, he had no reason to be suspicious.

Neither did Jessica; she'd never met him before. When she interviewed him, he was perfectly charming and his background checked out on an online search. In immediate need of an aide, she offered him the job.

Frankie and Vinny didn't know the guy either. They were in the dark when Arnie appeared in the living room. It was a testament to their trust in Bear that they'd acted so quickly to remove the blight.

But much to Arnie's surprise, Bear, Charlie, Eunice and I recognized the creep from our days at Soundside. He's the bastard who, you'll pardon my French, finger-fucked an old woman while we were all at Soundside. It happens, you know. Abuse of seniors. This guy was from a medical employment agency back then, a good worker, attractive, easy going. But in the night, he was a predator.

Mrs. Carlton had shared a room in the nursing home with Eunice. Long after dark, a struggle awakened my friend. When she saw what was going on, Eunice screamed and screamed until other aides and nurses arrived. Maybe Mrs. Carlton, whose dementia was extreme even back then, has recovered. But Eunice hasn't.

"It was awful. I had no idea anyone would do a thing like that, hold a helpless person down while he... she was crying and he was hurting her..." As her tears flowed, Frankie took her hand and whispered Italian nothings in her ear.

The rest of us hadn't recovered either, not really. The memory dredged up painful emotions for us all. Oh, what an awful time.

Jessica asked why the guy wasn't arrested. Her eyes were moist. Even Bear had to clear his throat before he answered her. "The director of the nursing home tried. He called the cops but Mrs. Carlton was too sick to say what happened to her. So no proof. Corporate headquarters and the placement agency conspired to cover it up. They fired the director in time because he wouldn't keep his mouth shut about it."

"But how does a jerkwad like Arnie Burgess pass the background checks to work at a nursing home?"

"Jess, you did your best. Unless he was actually convicted of a crime, a normal background check wouldn't find it. Without a conviction, an accusation - or even a plea bargain - won't stand."

"I'm so, so sorry, guys. How awful to come this close to bringing a monster in our midst."

I could see how bad she felt, how frightened. I told her that she took care of us every day. Sometimes, it felt good for us to take care of each other, too.

But in truth, the experience darkened the rest of the day. Earlier this evening, Eunice and I putted out to the barn in Sitting Bull. We stroked Burrito and Concha until we both felt better. And I noticed Bear cradling Baby Benny tonight while Charlie read with fat old Furball spread across his knees, purring up a storm.

Misery loves company.

Lily Gilbert, Cheerless Assistant to PI Bear Jacobs

They'd met twice in as many days. Yesterday they grabbed coffee after her work shift, although Keegan would have preferred a beer and a chance to wear something other than her uniform. Today, they walked the Edmonds beach before dinner at a waterfront restaurant known for its artistry with halibut, salmon, razor clams, oysters or whatever other seafood was in season.

She'd told him to call her Jo. Under no circumstances was he to refer to her as Cupcake. "That's my special hell from Bear," she said. "Since Bohannan is your name, I imagine people call you Bo. And since that rhymes with Jo, I just can't do it. Guess I'll stick with Doc."

He'd laughed. "Doc is good. Nobody's called me Bo since I was big enough to win my playground fights. What a name to saddle a kid with. Bohannon. Probably why I took to drink at an early age."

At dinner, she had wine but he ordered iced tea. She remembered then his earlier reference to drinking. After two hours of laughter and conversation every bit as fresh as the food, she asked, "You don't drink?"

"I drink too much," he answered. "But you make me want to think straight."

Poignant. But Jo knew too many boozer cops to want to hitch her wagon to a man with that crippling problem. And her judgment had been trampled on too recently to be very trusting of any man. Or at least her judgment of men. The worry of it cast a pall on a beautiful night, even on the kiss that was in every other way spectacular.

Go slow. Be sure of the path, her head cautioned her heart.

Shut the hell up, her heart answered.

The next morning, she called Jessica and had to put up with the caregiver's excitement about being a possible matchmaker. When Jess was done crowing and teasing, Jo turned serious. "Tell me about Doc."

"He's kind. Amazing with animals. People, too. He carried me when I didn't have the money to pay his bills on time. That helped get me started."

"Background?"

"Jo, I don't know much about that. Is this a criminal investigation? You're worse than the online match sites."

"I am. Does he drink?"

"He's Irish."

"I mean out of control."

"I've never seen him medicate an animal when he's too far gone, if that's what you mean. No surgery while soused. But, yes, I've smelled alcohol a time or two."

"And not the rubbing kind, I presume."

"Jo, quit being such a *cop*. Stop looking for evidence of suspicious behavior. You've had one dinner together. Give it a chance."

After the call, Keegan leaned back in her desk chair, propped her feet on the waste basket, and considered Jessica's wisdom. So the guy might be an animal rustler. And a serious boozer. But considerate. Kind was the word Jess used. Keegan could use a little of that caring treatment herself. *Maybe, just maybe it's worth a try*, she thought, as her head lost ground to the beat of her heart.

* * *

Bear *kachunked* into the living room and plopped down beside Lily. They hadn't talked since the Arnie fiasco that morning. He'd denned up a couple of hours to sulk. The retired private investigator always had a strong sense of justice, although maybe his own definition of it more than the law's. Now, in his later years, justice for seniors was a mission.

He knew his crew was a physically decrepit lot, just a few ticks above morgue patrons on the death scale. Lily had lost a leg to diabetes, Charlie was wheelchair bound, Eunice's heart danced to a beat of its own, Frankie quietly suffered Parkinson's, and he himself needed the quad cane to move from point A to point B.

"Open your computer," he said to Lily once he settled.

"Glad to see you, too, Bear."

"We have work to do. I have a plan."

She opened the Toshiba. "A plan involving removing the balls from nursing aide Arnie Burgess?"

"How did you know?"

"It's scary how often we think alike."

"That fucker got away with it last time. We need to stop him," Bear said, as much to himself as to Lily.

"Will we get help from Keegan?"

"Nope. Still no proof. And she can't do much. Sometimes it's a pain that she's such an honest cop."

The Toshiba sounded its ready-to-go riff. "Okay. Where to?"

"I want to know where he lives. So we start with finding the address of the Beetle owner. I got the license number before he drove away." Bear directed her to a site that he used in his days as a private investigator.

"Couldn't we just ask Jessica to see his employment application?"

"Yes. But it's just as well she doesn't know we're looking for him 'til we have a plan."

The address appeared on the screen. Bear looked over her shoulder and said, "Hmmm. An apartment number. South of here. Make a note of that. Case we need it."

Lily complied. Then she enthused, "Oh! We can make a list of all the nursing homes in, say, a five mile area of his digs. And we can contact every one of them with a be-on-the-lookout."

Good idea. But there might be an easier way to pinpoint him. I called Will. Asked him about yesterday when Arnie came for his interview."

"What did he have to say?"

27

"Arnie told Will he was back in town after a time out of state. If he didn't get the job here, he had an interview this week at Gardenview Estates Elder Care. Not far from here."

"So we call them and tell them not to hire the son of a bitch."

"I tried. They told me they don't share information regarding employment with private investigators."

"Especially retired ones?" Lily wasn't above sarcasm, which he considered one of her best traits unless it was aimed at him.

"Lily, our job is to get information, not share information about unimportant things like retirement."

"So we go in guns blazing 'til they listen."

Bear smiled at her. "You sound like Eunice."

"No. *Snuff da sucka* sounds like Eunice."

This time, Bear went all the way to a chuckle before saying, "I'm thinking more along the lines of surveillance. We watch for him for the rest of the week. See if he keeps his interview with them. If he does, we make a scene in their lobby if we have to."

"Okay. I'm in. How do we handle it?"

"Sitting Bull. Oh, and you tell Jessica."

* * *

While Bear worked out the logistics for the surveillance, Lily talked with Jessica. It was surprisingly simple to convince the caregiver that stakeout-by-golf-cart was a good idea.

"Something's up with that. It was too easy," Lily said to Eunice.

"Oh, I don't know. Maybe she thinks this caper needs to be done, unlike some of Bear's other schemes."

"Well, maybe."

They were at the library, sitting side by side in front of the public computers, speaking in hushed voices, and putting an email blast together. Eunice was delighted to be involved with what she called the Strike Against That Shit. While Lily composed a post, Eunice used Google to locate emails for elder care facilities in the area.

The subject line was PREDATOR ON THE LOOSE. Lily dropped in the photo of Arnie from Bear's phone, having cropped out as much of Vinny as she could. Arnie looked as though a disembodied arm was around his neck, strangling him.

Next she typed: *Arnie Burgess is a known sex offender. He has committed elder abuse before and is looking for work where he can do it again. Please do not endanger your residents by employing this man.*

Eunice whispered, "I think it's libel even if we're sure it's true."

"Maybe. But they have to know who sent it."

Sam had driven them to the library to use the computers instead of Lily's laptop. He agreed to do it if Eunice would mend a shirt for him. After she composed her list, Eunice repaired a three-corner tear while Lily sent the emails.

Eunice fretted. "It won't reach everybody. Lots of places don't list as elder care."

"True. But it'll be many. There," Lily said with a final tappity-tap flourish. "At least they've been told. Whether they ignore it or not is up to them."

29

* * *

Cognition wasn't a problem for Bear's gang, but locomotion was. To increase their physical reach, they had Sitting Bull. The souped-up golf cart was candy apple red and big enough for four passengers complete with walkers and wheels. It was street worthy, with all the bells and whistles to make it legal on roads posted at 35 mph. Of course, it damn near internally hemorrhaged at 30, and even Jessica had to admit that wasn't fast enough for them to run into too much trouble. Well, it wasn't likely anyway. Of course, she didn't know that Bear's driver license had run out. It was that kind of minor detail he didn't worry about.

Early the next morning, Bear and Lily putted to Gardenview Estates. They arrived by nine, assuming nobody scheduled an interview before that time of day. Or later than five. They were prepared to wait the eight hours with an igloo cooler of water and a packed lunch from Aurora. And eight hours again the next day if necessary.

"Has a fancy entrance but no garden in sight," Bear said, assessing the property. The portico stuck straight out, tall and imposing, as though the place was a mansion. But the building itself wasn't fooling anybody.

"Not much of an estate, either."

Assuming Sitting Bull would draw too much attention in the parking lot, they parked across the road, under an obliging willow tree whose branches shielded them from the sun and partially obscured them from the Gardenview portico. Not that an oversized cart, red as a baboon's ass, was ever quite invisible.

"They'll see us," Lily said, peering through an old pair of binoculars. "How do you focus these damn things?"

"Maybe they'll see us," Bear replied, stifling a laugh as Lily twisted the focus button to and fro. "But we aren't on their property so why would they care?"

Lily repeated Bear's plan aloud. "Just to review: when we see the orange Beetle, we race to the front door and demand to see the administrator. Right?"

"Race?"

"Well, okay. Putt. If they do nothing and we have to make a scene, we do it. We stop Arnie Burgess from working here. If they hire him anyway, we picket."

"Correct."

Appearing to have the binoculars under control at last, she scanned the parking lot. "Hey," she said, sitting up straight.

"Hey what?"

"That car. In the lot. The big -"

"- butt Caddy? Black and sleek? Yep. It's Vinny. Got here ahead of us."

Lily snorted. "Vinny is surveilling us surveilling the nursing home?"

"That's how it appears."

"So *that's* why Jess didn't throw a hissy when I told her the plan. She knew she'd ask Frankie's thug to stake us out. I'll be damned."

"Should we be mad? Not to be treated as independent, competent seniors, and all that? Should we pout?" Bear pulled down the corners of his mouth in a mock frown.

"Hell no."

"I agree. Damn glad he's here."

The two old friends sat in the cart until midday. By then, Bear was desperate to pee. "Used to hold it longer in the old days of stakeouts," Bear lamented.

"Used to do a lot of things better back then."

They drove Sitting Bull to the portico. First Lily went in, bold as a visitor, and found a restroom. Bear followed. When they came out, Bear drove Sitting Bull into the parking lot.

"Not going back to the tree?"

"Nope. If he's gonna sit here, we're sitting with him. Might not be as fun as a golf cart, but the Caddy's a lot more comfortable on these old bones."

They placed the golf cart on the street side of the Caddy, away from the portico. Vinny got out to help them both into the car's back seat. He wasn't much of a talker, and they saw no reason to say anything either.

The afternoon passed slowly, especially once Bear started humming oldies like *Darktown Strutters Ball* followed by *Wait for the Wagon* and *On the Road to Mandalay*. He tried to think of other road trip songs, but Lily refused to help.

* * *

"The Irish make very little that's worth eating," Doc said. "But stew and soda bread are pretty darn good." His kitchen was warm from the oven and stovetop. Other than spoons and knives he'd been using, the whole place was spotless although everything could use updating, the laminate counters to the linoleum floor.

Keegan's bar stool sat on one side of the counter as Doc worked on the other. She thought she'd drool as he popped a crusty loaf out of the cast iron skillet where it had been cooling. He sliced it and set it on the kitchen counter, next to a warm plate of butter. Then he placed a bowl of stew in front of her, a concoction he'd thickened with mashed potatoes.

"This is mutton. Think of it as an adventure if you've never had it. One of the local farmers pays his vet bill in organic meat."

No guts, no glory, she thought as she nibbled a small piece of meat. Stringy and stinky had been her guess. But she was wrong.

"My goodness. This is delicious!" The surprise was genuine and so was his smile as she forked a larger bite.

He set large mugs of tea next to each of their servings, and he joined her on a neighboring stool. "I have a bottle of red if you prefer."

"Not very Irish, though, is it?" she asked, glad the subject was broached. She had questions for him.

"Well, not very *me*, at least." Doc broke a piece of bread, buttered it, then dipped it into his bowl. "I don't drink, Jo, because I can't. Alcoholic. Took me years to admit it, say it out loud, and finally do something about it. I've been sober for a year and two weeks."

She was relieved she wouldn't have to outright ask. "Amazing. I know a lotta cops who haven't been able to control it. Good for you."

He shrugged. "Maybe I can't either. I've never seen a wagon that you couldn't fall off. But this is who I am now, and who I hope to be in the future. No guarantees. But I'm fighting." He stared at her. "You need to know that before we go any further."

It couldn't be plainer than that. He wouldn't promise what he couldn't promise. Maybe she fell a little bit in love right then for that honesty. At least this time, she knew the potential for hurt was there. It wouldn't come as a malicious, blindsiding surprise.

"I think the next step is for me to cook," she said. "It's only fair you know how awful that can be."

* * *

The next morning, Sitting Bull stayed home on its plug, and Vinnie drove them to Gardenview Estates. This time Eunice came along for the ride and updated them on happenings at Latin's Ranch the day before.

"Yesterday, Sam emptied the shed and put a tarp over the stuff he hauled outside. He's building four stalls in there. One for the burros, one for Gina Lola, two for whatever Doc brings next. Latin's Farm is underway."

"Good on Sam," Lily said.

"And Charlie's up to his elbows helping out. Sam says he's a good handyman."

"What's he doing?"

"When I was in the shed, he installed hinges and latches on all the gates. Then he pushed his wheelchair up to a workbench to sand boards Sam cut for mangers. I helped, too. Washed some curry brushes Jessica donated. Installed hooks for leads and halters on one of the walls. Hmm...maybe I'll macramé some really fancy leads."

"Has anyone stopped by, asking questions? Farmers looking for burro banditos?" Bear asked.

"No one. Nothing in the local blat about lost burros either. So far, so good."

"Guess if you don't care for an animal, you don't care much what happens to it," Lily said.

"Maybe, maybe not. An owner, even a bad one, likes to make that decision for himself," Bear said. He didn't want the others to lose all sense of caution about the two little beasts.

After that, conversation lulled as they silently waited. Lily opened her laptop so she could do the crossword online with no input from Bear. She'd packed along her headphones, too, in case he decided to hum.

* * *

At eleven, Bear huffed. "Well, I'll be." He watched a woman exit the front door of Gardenview. His eye was drawn as it always was to redheads. She still had the gams of a dancer although her body was thickened, that of a fit but older woman. The wild red curls pulled back by some arcane hair-holding device allowed him to see the gray at the roots. As she neared the Caddy, Bear exited the front seat. He grabbed his cane and *kachunked* in her direction.

"Hey, Ginger," he said.

She stopped. The wrinkles that lined her eyes intensified as she focused on him. It was a frowny stare of concentration until she finally exclaimed, "The shamus! You old son of a bitch." Her face lit up with a smile far more knowing than the Mona Lisa.

Ginger took his hand, the one free of his quad cane. She held it a moment longer than necessary. This woman had helped him before. Ginger was the waitress at a cop bar called the Abbey when Bear discovered it was a drop for snuff films; Frankie's gang had closed it down. Most of the patrons and staff never knew the whole story.

"Where you working now?" Bear asked.

"The Abbey wasn't the only cop bar on the beat. The gang there moved on to the Irishman. Some of us were glad of your help. Might be a free beer in it for you and your sidekick, what was his name, Horse."

Bear laughed. He'd forgotten that Horse Smith was the alias he'd given Sam Hart in the heat of the moment. "We'll be sure to do that." He motioned with his head to the Gardenview portico. "You have people here?"

"My ma. Won't be long," she said with a sigh. Her Irish eyes clouded. "How 'bout you?"

Bear told her about Arnie Burgess. As the story rolled, she looked more and more appalled until her jaw actually dropped. By the end of Bear's tale, she snapped her mouth shut, then opened those plumb red lips just enough to hiss, "That scum. Might have to tell a few of my patrons about him. Some cops need less proof than others to see a guy gets a one way ticket outta town. Is my ma safe for now?"

"That's why we're here." He indicated the Caddy and was glad she couldn't actually see through the tinted glass. Let her imagine a gang of desperados instead of a gang of Lily and Eunice. "If Arnie shows here, he won't stay long. Just a sec." He frisked himself until he found an ancient steno-type notebook in a back pocket. "Got a pen?"

She quickly unearthed one from her purse. Bear made a note of Arnie's address, ripped it from the spiral and handed it to her. "Maybe your friends would like to pay him a visit one night soon. Maybe tonight."

After Bear said goodbye to Ginger and folded himself back into the front seat of the Caddy, one bestie in the back asked, "What was that about?"

The other added, "You have some 'splainin' to do."

CHAPTER FOUR

Case Notes
June 8, 10 a.m.

Soon after Ginger switched her hips out of the lot (not that I think she looked a little long in the tooth for that strut or those boobs or anything), and Bear had explained their conversation, a pock-marked orange Beetle chugged into the Gardenview parking lot.

"Head's up," said Bear.

Vinny answered, "My head is not down, Signore Bear." Gotta love the guy.

"I mean he's here, *Vinny. The VW. Let's move to the portico. Get ahead of him."*

When the game is afoot, we all let Bear take the lead. Only one commander when the chips are down, right? But heaven help him order us around in any other circumstance.

At the portico, Bear sent Eunice inside to plead the case against hiring Arnie Burgess who was about to enter for his interview. He figured she was the nicest of us. Not sure that's true but appearances can deceive. It was easy to overlook the tough woman under that orange spiky hair, fluttering kaftan and puff of designer scent. But Eunice was out for blood when it came to this shameful aide. I felt a little sorry for the Gardenview receptionist.

While Eunice wafted into the reception area, we stayed out front, Bear, Vinny and me. It wasn't exactly going to be the gunfight at the OK Corral. We weren't armed or anything. Well, I wasn't. Bear does have that stiletto hidden in his cane, and Vinny clanks like a mobile armory. So I guess it could have been a gunfight. And I suppose Arnie could be carrying. Never mind about that not-being-armed thing.

Arnie wasn't paying much attention as he walked toward us. Seen one old geezer, you've seen them all, right? At least until one of them calls you an asshole and the other says you're a dirtbag.

Arnie halted. Not sure Bear and I stopped him. But when he eyed Vinny, I thought he might run. I give him some credit for standing his ground. Brave or a fool.

"What the fuck is up with you people? What have I ever done to you?"

"Not a thing to us. But we aren't Olivia Carlton," I said.

"Who the hell is that?"

"Resident at Soundside while you were there," Bear answered.

I couldn't match Bear's deep growl, but I did my best to sound disgusted. "What you did to her is unforgivable."

Gears must have slowly meshed in Arnie's noggin. "You mean all that fuss that got me in such trouble? None of that shit was true."

"Our friend Eunice saw it happen."

"Yeah, well she keeps spreading rumors, she better watch out what might happen to her."

Three things occurred at once.

Vinny pounced forward. Frankie would never forgive him if he didn't castrate any bastard who threatened the capo's little dove.

Bear yelled, "Vinny, no! Don't kill him!" and thrust himself in front of the charging mobster.

As that pile of manhood hit the ground wrapped up together, I grabbed Bear's cane and smacked it over Arnie's head. He crumpled beside the first two, then stayed put, appearing dazed. Meanwhile, Vinny assisted Bear to his feet, and I gave him back his cane. He brushed himself off, straightened his shirt over his belly, and claimed to be unhurt.

That's when Arnie began to move. I hadn't knocked him out, but I figure he'll feel a goose egg for a week or two. "We're watching for you, Arnie. Stay clear of our part of town from now on."

He stood with a grunt and a wobble. Then the four of us stared at each other like dingos circling a bone.

That's when Gardenview's electric door whooshed open and Eunice appeared alongside a tight-lipped woman who looked like Management to me. Her face was a worrisome red, like her blood was boiling. "Get out of here, all of you. We're not hiring anyone today." She stared malevolence at Arnie then turned on us. "And we certainly aren't looking for residents who behave like you do." She turned on her heel and departed, the door whooshing closed behind her. When it clicked we knew she had locked us out.

Eunice finally had the chance to have her say to Arnie. I thought she would level him to the ground again. But she didn't use any ass-burning language at all. Instead, she sounded deeply sad. "You are pathetic. There is no place and no one on this earth who will ever want you near them. How alone you are."

She turned and went to the Caddy. Bear stood tall on his cane and held my arm as we strolled back to the car, as well. I don't know what Vinny said to Arnie, but the young man, rubbing his head, limped to his Beetle and disappeared before the Caddy oozed out of the lot toward home.

Lily Gilbert, Relieved Assistant to PI Bear Jacobs

Jo Keegan thought of herself as an exacting peace officer when it came to defending the law. She'd seen crime so malicious it would make anyone cynical about the worth of the entire human race. Nonetheless, she protected the accused and the victim alike.

Except now. She was absolutely sure this farmer had a right to claim the burros. But she was equally sure he had no right to starve animals or yell at her friends.

She arrived after Doc; the two planned to rent a couple of Jessica's horses for a trail ride. She stopped as she entered the barn, hearing Jessica say, "You've been offered a fair price which is more than you deserve."

Eunice, with Lily in Sitting Bull, agreed. "I'm willing to pay for the burros."

The rawboned man in denims rasped, "You bet you'll pay, old woman. Five thousand apiece oughta do it."

"That's robbery." Jessica squawked.

"Look who's talking," the farmer sneered back. His stance was aggressive, but so was Jessica's.

"You don't want them. You don't even feed them." Lily said, sounding reasonable.

"Useless little shits. Pay up or I go to the law."

So much for reasonable, Keegan thought.

Doc stepped into the battle. "Oh, come on, Buzz. You do that, and I'll have to tell the police about the other abused animals on your prop - "

The farmer rounded on the vet. "You threaten me and I'll ruin you with the other - "

Keegan stepped forward, shouting over the fray, "Anybody here has anything to say to the law, here I am."

Silence. The air crackled with anger from two senior residents, one caregiver, one vet and one farmer. The farmer opened his yap for another snarl.

"BEWHEAWHEAWHEAH." Burrito broke the moment. The farmer issued a final invective to them and their mothers alike, then stomped from the barn with his hands over his ears.

"Is there anything going on here I should know about?" Keegan asked into the sudden silence.

"No, ma'am," Eunice and Lily said, turning Sitting Bull to leave the scene.

"Gosh, no," Jessica said. "I'm just in the barn choosing the two best horses for you and Doc. Now let's see..." She walked away, down the row of stalls.

Only Doc came toward Keegan. "That's one mad farmer, but he'll cool down. Buzz isn't a bad guy. And he sure doesn't want what he calls useless mouths to feed. You were here in the nick of time, just like the Mounties in old movies."

Keegan smiled at him and moved another step closer. From this distance, chests touching, she had to look up. "And like the Mounties, Doc, I always get my man."

* * *

It was a week later that Sam drove Bear to the Irishman. Ginger delivered two pints with an, "On the House."

"Arnie Burgess seems to have disappeared," Bear said to the waitress. "We've called every nursing facility in the area and no sign of him."

"We do drive-bys of his apartment but never see his VW," Sam added. "No lights on, either."

"Well, I have friends, Horse. Some of them in this very place."

The quizzical look on Sam's face indicated he'd also forgotten his alias. "Horse?" he mouthed to Bear.

She ignored Horse since she was also looking at Bear. "And they didn't like to think of my dear old ma in danger."

Bear nodded. "Someone might have paid him a visit?"

"Could be. Could be." She sashayed away to the next table.

Sam took a sip of the rich lager. "I'd say the area is safer for seniors than it was last week. Another case closed, Bear."

Bear, never one for overly happy endings, said, "It's just one bad apple amongst many, Sam." Then he lifted his glass in a toast. "But it's a start."

THREE BEARS

A BEARABLE EXIT

THREE BEARS

A BEARABLE EXIT

CHAPTER ONE

Case Notes
August 30, 10 a.m.

Autumn smells sharp and crisp as an apple, not soft like the sweet scents of summer. It warns of biting things to come, cold rain and shortened days. But this late August morning was still warm. I was pruning the last of the Gentle Hermione roses in their fat ginger jar planters. My nose was snuffled amidst them to catch enough of their glorious scent to last me through the winter.

Bear, at the patio table, blew on his coffee while he flipped through the newspaper. Next to him, Eunice was beading some damn thing. Neither Charlie nor Frankie had appeared yet to join us after breakfast. But our caregiver, Jessica, sat legs akimbo on the patio, brushing out Folly's spaniel/dachshund coat. She called the little dog her cockadock.

47

"Oh quit with the big drippy eyes," she said. "I'm not hurting you."

Folly whimpered and rolled the aforementioned eyes once more.

Jessica answered Folly's question. "No, Good Fella is not *getting off scot free. He's next in line." At the moment, the gangly Husky pup was scratching his back on the grass with four paws, one long tongue, and naughty bits lolling skyward.*

"HELP!" Charlie's old voice crackled from the house, shattering the peace. "JESSICA! It's Frankie. He's fallen."

Jessica leapt like a gazelle, virtually levitating into the house. Even so, Vinny the bodyguard beat her to the old mobster from wherever he'd been lurking.

Long before the rest of us arrived on our walkers and wheels, we could hear the don imploring Vinny to lift him. "Nobody see me in this way." By nobody, I'm guessing he especially meant Eunice. His little dove.

"He was on his walker, and next thing I knew, he was on the ground," yelped Charlie, approaching panic pitch in a voice that was too high to begin with. The dogs must be shuddering. "Just fell over like a tree. I mean a falling tree. Timber. Just fell over..."

"Stop babbling, Charlie. We got the idea." It sounded gruff, but I saw Bear put his paw on Charlie's narrow shoulder and give it a pat.

Vinny picked Frankie up as easily as I would gather a fallen leaf.

Jessica was calling 911 when Frankie murmured, "No, Signora. Vinny, he take me to our medico." Even in a whisper, an order from the don sounded as serious as an eleventh commandment.

Of course Frankie would have a doctor of his own. Someone who owed the mob. Someone discreet who would not tell the world how fragile the old boss was.

Jessica was brought up short but not completely buffaloed. "Okay. But I'm coming, too. Chrissie, you're on watch," she said to our favorite aide who nodded as she began shooing the rest of us out of the way. We'd gathered around to offer whatever support a pack of octogenarians can muster.

Vinny carried Frankie out to the Caddy and arranged him in the back seat. Jessica jumped in next to the don where she would no doubt irritate the crap out of him with her attentive fussing. Vinny, bodyguard cum chauffeur, lost no time maneuvering the big car up the driveway and away.

The rest of us sat in the living room which was too quiet and too empty. Frankie should have been in the space on the sofa next to Eunice. It looked as though Death had paid us a visit.

To stop that line of thought, I occupied the spot myself. "He'll be okay, Eunice. He's a tough old bird." I would have held her hand, but she was still clutching her beadwork. Her knuckles were so white it appeared sharp bones poked through her tissue-thin skin.

She didn't answer me, only nodded. For all her silliness, Eunice is no dumb bunny. She's seen pain. She's felt grief. Plenty of it. She'd steeled herself against making a breast-beating scene. In a soft but steady voice she said, "He has Parkinson's, you know."

Lily Gilbert, Sad Assistant to PI Bear Jacobs

"He has Parkinson's, you know."

Lily knew, and probably Bear did, too; nothing much got past him. It was Charlie who seemed blindsided. "Parkinson's? Oh Eunice. I know it's bad, but what does that mean? What will happen to him?"

"Well, Charlie, simply put, his brain is dying. Bad cells are destroying the good. It's been going on for quite some time."

Eunice got the words out, but nothing more. She sewed the razzle-dazzle beads to a strip of Spandex in swift, measured stitches.

"If his brain is dying, does that mean the don is dying?" Subtlety was not Charlie's strong suit.

Lily sighed. "It probably means that, yes, Charlie. There is no cure, but some treatments can really help. Frankie has lots of good days ahead." She knew it wasn't likely to be true. She had lived through a nursing home and looked death in the face through diseased eyes of her own. People who'd done that knew a pipe dream from a nightmare. Frankie's hand tremors would work their way up his arms, walking would get harder for him than it already was, balance and memory would be lost along with all body control. Lily wondered if she'd said hopeful words to Charlie because he needed to hear them or because she did.

The four old friends sat quietly for a long time. Lily saw Eunice's tears plop onto the aqua Spandex, although that plucky old lady never made a sound. Bear worked the newspaper's crossword puzzle that he'd gotten to before Lily nabbed it.

Lily opened her Toshiba and began another case note. She also watched Charlie roll his wheelchair to the game table and begin painting wooden rings in bright colors. It was a task that Frankie had been doing for Eunice's most recent craft extravaganza. Charlie must have decided to pick up the slack. He might be a womanizing, self-centered nincompoop, but that didn't mean he was without kindness.

At lunchtime, the cook, Aurora, did not demand their presence in the dining room. Lily knew this highly unusual act was out of love. Aurora looked at the presentation of her meals as the highlight of anybody's day, but she must have acknowledged their sorrow for Frankie. Instead of rousting them to the table, she let Chrissie bring them each a TV tray with a bowl of manicotti casserole, the cheese on the Italian sausage and noodles bubbling hot and brown. It was a recipe that Frankie had shared with Aurora. The don and she, arguing every step of the way, had perfected a variety of cuisine they called Mexi-Sicilian. It was Latin's Ranch comfort food.

Lily grieved. Frankie was more than a retired don who loved her bestie, Eunice. He was a load-bearing wall for most of them at Latin's Ranch. At one time or another, they all benefited from his company and largesse. She'd known of his illness, but when it lay dormant for so long before raising its ugly head again, it was easy to forget how dangerous that snake in the grass could be.

A product of the Sicilian male-driven society, Frankie Sapienza nonetheless accepted Lily as an intelligence not to be trifled with. And he gave Bear near *familia* status as a solver of problems and crimes. Frankie looked past their age, non-Italian-ness, and physical weaknesses to hone in on their brains. He helped them feel vital, alive.

If there was any way Lily could use her brain power to help this old man as his life came to its conclusion, well, by holy hell, she would.

* * *

Frankie, Jessica and Vinny returned mid-afternoon. The don apologized for worrying them, then asked Vinny to take him to his room.

As far as anyone knew, Eunice had never been to Frankie's room. While she was immune to society's dictates, the don would never compromise a lady by inviting her into his domain *privato*. Nevertheless, this time Eunice insisted. Bear heard her say to Vinny, "You try to keep me out, and I'll slap you senseless before you can find your brass knuckles."

Bear rumbled, his version of a chuckle.

Jessica told the rest what they wanted to know. Yes, the Parkinson's was active, and yes, she would be keeping a close eye on Frankie from now on. She huffed, "That doctor said Latin's Ranch could be his home only until he requires more care than we can give."

"He said that to you?" *Brave doctor*, Bear thought, *or a damn fool*.

"Can you imagine? Frankie isn't just mob *familia*. He's Latin's Ranch family, too." She marched off toward her office, or the upstairs where her husband Ben was keeping an eye on Baby Benny, or to the barn to talk with the nags. Bear wasn't sure which, but those were the three spots she went for comfort. Jessica was predictable that way.

When she was out of earshot, Charlie asked, "Do you suppose that means she'd never kick any of us out, either?"

"No, Charlie," Bear answered. "She'd kick your sorry ass to the curb in a heartbeat."

"You're being unbearable, Bear," Lily sniped. "Now hand over the front page."

"Okay. And here's the finished crossword if you'd like to look at the answers."

* * *

Frankie did not appear until after dinner. He looked refreshed, rosy-skinned and hale, as he and Eunice joined Bear and Lily on the patio to watch the sunset. Charlie departed to see reruns of *Charlie's Angels*, the original one. He was a purist about that. "Farrah Fawcett kinda ruined me for other angels," he told them as he wheeled away.

"Good to see you, Frankie," Bear said. "Feeling better? You're looking better."

"Like stallion. Italian stallion."

Lily thought Frankie looked good but not that good.

"I wish to have conversation with Vinny gone from room. So I say to him, go away."

"He's worried about you. We all are. Go easy on us while we take care of you." Eunice batted her false eyelashes. "It's so often the other way around. You caring for us."

"No cause for concern, my little dove. But things need done I do not wish him to hear. I wish to tell you, Signora Lily."

"Me? Well, okay. Sure." Lily could not imagine what the don would have to say to her that Vinny couldn't hear.

"Es your daughter, a fine lady."

"Ah." Now Lily *could* imagine. Maybe the don had noticed that Sylvia carried an Olympic-sized torch for his bodyguard, Vinny. What becomes of a woman who gets between a don and his thug? Would he have her whacked?

"Ah," she repeated, at a loss for anything more useful to say.

"My Vinny? He love your daughter."

"Ah." So Vinny was the issue here, not Sylvia. Vinny would be the one sleeping with fishes.

"Your daughter, she es friend of my grandson, Antonio."

Okay where is this going? Yes, his Antonio was Sylvia's Tony. The gay lover of her husband. Well, when her husband was still alive. Lily looked from Bear to Eunice. Were they keeping up? She sure as hell wasn't. Carefully, she said, "Yes, Sylvia has become very close to Tony. They have helped each other through difficult times."

"This I know. He was lover of her husband."

Even Eunice gave a little gasp. "You mean you *knew* Tony is gay?"

Everybody else knew Tony was gay, but they'd always tiptoed around the subject when Frankie was in range. Celebrating the rainbow flag just wasn't the *familia* way.

Frankie turned adoring eyes toward Eunice and explained he was aware of Tony's preferences. He was old-fashioned but not that old-fashioned. "Es nice you try to save this news from me."

Lily asked, "But what does this have to do with Sylvia?"

Frankie said, "Tony must prepare to be head of *familia* now as Angel of Death draws near for me."

Lily gulped and shot a look at Eunice.

"It's all right, Lily. Frankie and I are well aware that days are numbered."

Okay...but does Tony know he's about to be made the boss? Would he accept? Could he refuse? And what does that mean to Sylvia? Lily was so far in the dark, she could have been mining coal. "I'm glad you are prepared for what lies ahead, Frankie. But how is Tony's, ah, promotion related to my daughter?"

"Antonio must go to Italy and Sicily now. Meet...people of importance. See his homeland."

Lily guessed Tony thought the USA was his homeland, but whatever.

Frankie continued. For a man who seldom spoke, this was a helluva monologue. "Antonio has much to learn before he runs businesses of *familia*."

Go ahead and say it. Rackets, Lily thought.

"I must send Tony, and he must have protection," Frankie said. "I trust nobody but Vinny to do this."

"Uh-huh." The bodyguard clanged with weaponry. His muscles stretched sleeves to the snapping point. Of course, Frankie would trust him to look out for his grandson. "But..."

"You do not see, *Signora* Lily?"

"Yeah. For a PI's assistant, you're being pretty slow on the uptake, Lily." Bear was red in the face, that snotty look when he was holding back a laugh. Lily shot him a stink eye.

Frankie went on. "Tony must have wife. I accept his inclination, but this does not mean all *familia* does so. Tony, he likes your daughter. He will pretend she es his wife."

"He what? Bear, did you know about this?" She narrowed her eyes.

Mr. Innocent lifted his shoulders in a shrug at the mystery of it all. It didn't fool Lily for a second.

"But Vinny loves your daughter. He wishes to marry her. This could be problem but es now blessing. Vinny will be real husband. Then he goes with them, and *familia* in Sicily think she es wife of Tony, but she es secret wife of Vinny. Everyone es happy. *Capisce?*"

"*Capisce*? No *capisce*! No *capisce*! Why would Sylvia go along with that?"

Bear interrupted. "Let's see if I got this. Sylvia is Tony's friend but she lusts after Vinny. This way she gets them both. Right, Frankie?"

"*Sì, naturalmente*. Antonio and Vinny do this for me because they honor me. Sylvia do this for you because you are her mother, dear Lily."

Bear added, "You wish her good luck, right, Lily? She gets both guys, plus I'm guessing it's no small thing to have the don be grateful."

Lily looked at him open-mouth, then turned to Frankie. "But Sylvia is her own person. Middle-aged, or near enough. Owns a business. Has a mind of her own." Lily realized her hands were flapping like a vulture's wings near roadkill.

"You are her mother, *Signore* Lily. She obey you, yes?"

Lily felt heat rising fast, her inner caldron about to spit all over the stove.

Bear appeared to hide a guffaw with an ursine-size cough. "I think, Frankie, Lily may be a little taken aback at the moment. Women can find new ideas so challenging. My advice? Give her a bit of time."

Lily sputtered. "You...I...she..."

Frankie turned gratefully to Bear. "As usual, you are correct at solving puzzle. I allow time for this thought to blossom like flower for mother and daughter." He sighed, clearly tired after so much talk. "But not too much time."

CHAPTER TWO

Case Notes
August 30, 9 p.m.

I hate being out-maneuvered. Who the hell doesn't? So I'm mighty mad at that meddling manipulator, Bear Jacobs (sorry about the ems...alliteration seems to happen when I'm pissed).

As soon as Eunice and Frankie went off to join Charlie for television, I wiped the shit-eating smile off the insufferable shamus' smoocher (sorry, again...I'll quit now). "How long have you known about this?"

Bear blinked, feigning surprise at my attack. But his beady eyes shone like obsidian. "Gosh, Lily, Frankie just took a turn for the worse this morning. How old could his plan be?"

"Don't dodge the question. How long have you known about this?"

"Calm yourself. It's only natural the don is thinking about the future as the Angel of Death swoops closer to..."

"HOW LONG HAVE YOU KNOWN ABOUT THIS?"

"You sound like a parrot."

"Then speak up before I crack your pinkie with my beak."

He caved under my hard-core interrogation techniques.

"Okay, okay. The don may have mentioned his wishes for a Tony/Vinnie/ Sylvia mash-up. It's possible I remember such a thing. I know he's been thinking about the future of his family for some time, with his grandson at the helm."

Tony as top mobster? *"Where's Tony's father? Why not him?"*

I saw a genuine shiver wobble Bear's cheeks. *"You're kidding, right? You don't expect me to ask Frankie a question like that."*

He had a point. What happens in Moblandia stays in Moblandia. *"No. I suppose not."* I took a deep breath. Then another.

Bear leaned back and crossed his hands over his ample belly. *"Okay, Lily. Frankie has had a word or three with me, now and then, in the past few months. He's been feeling fragile for a while."*

"So you are a creator of this harebrained scheme?"

"No. Yes. I mean, okay, I might have helped him organize his thoughts. But Lily." He bent ever so slightly closer to me. That meant he was serious. *"Is it really so harebrained?"*

Bear is smart. Damn smart about the law, ethics, police, outlaws. But I fear the heart of a woman is a heart of darkness to him.

"Yes. It is harebrained. Sylvia would be appalled."

"Are you sure...or is it you who is appalled?" He held up his big paws as if to fend off my next volley. *"Before you reject it, give it a little thought. She loves Vinny; she's told me that. And Tony is her best friend; she's told you that. She likes to be with them both. Is this charade really so bad? Might she not enjoy it?"*

"At the risk of sounding like a parrot again, Sylvia would be appalled."

"But if she wants a virile man, one who worships her, why not Vinny? And isn't Tony her travel companion? Her BFF, I believe it is called. Why does that have to change? They can enjoy fashion

shows while Vinny takes in gun shows. What's so wrong with that for a spirited lady of some years who has had a hard time of it?"

Boy, wouldn't Sylvia just love that description. But, damn him, he had a point. She wasn't a child bound by any rules. Other than my own, that is, since I'm her mother.

"Are you really so sure she'd be appalled?"

I felt my eyes narrow once again as the penny dropped through my gumball machine. He'd already talked with Sylvia about this! Was she...

At that very second, Will Haverstock arrived and flopped onto a lawn chair in a sweaty rawboned pile of arms and legs. Good Fella leapt on his lap. "Wow! This pup can run. Three miles and he isn't even panting. You ready to hit the hay, Bear?"

"You bet," Bear said. "Right now! You're in the nick of time to lend a hand."

Normally I love this dear boy, Will. He's Chrissie's beau, filling in until Jessica can replace Rick. But at the moment I wanted to beak him, too, for forcing me to postpone the rest of this chat until tomorrow.

I hate to be out-maneuvered.

     Lily Gilbert, Manipulated Assistant to PI Bear Jacobs

Sylvia Henderson made her decision days before Lily was told about Frankie's plan. The don had informed his grandson, and Bear, a very uncomfortable matchmaker, had approached Sylvia. Both old men believed they'd have better luck getting what Frankie wanted if Lily was last to know. Bear said to Sylvia, "I'll pay for that decision. One way or another, Lily will get me for it." Sylvia had no doubt of that.

Tony and she worked it out through several walks on the beach, a handful of debates, and more glasses of wine than she cared to count. Now they were agreed. But they needed to confirm with each other daily lest one of them back out. It was an earth-moving, mind-bending, ethics-probing decision that could not be reversed once it was set in motion.

Sylvia was glad she'd been given time to consider it before Lily was involved. And Lily was the reason for that, although she could never know the whole truth. Frankie promised Sylvia that the mob would care for Lily for all time, anything she needed. Eunice, Bear, and Charlie, too. It was an offer that truly was hard to refuse. Sylvia's resources weren't unlimited. If one of the old gang had to go back to a nursing home or face serious surgery? Well, it didn't bear thinking about. The mob might well be a godsend.

But what about her own feelings? No doubt Vinny loved her. He'd proposed often enough. He just wanted to wait for marriage to seal the deal. Sylvia learned with Kyle that love could be more about affection than passion. But now...this time...what if sex was the eye- popping, bell-ringing lust of movies and books? Did that really exist?

Sylvia wanted to give it a go at least once in her life. And nobody on earth weakened her knees like Vinny. Now in her forties, she wanted to waste no more time. Wasn't it crazy for her to balk at the idea of a little thing like wedding vows?

Was the deception only a guise for the length of the trip, or was it for good? Maybe the three of them would pretend Tony and she were the couple even when they came back home. Vinny and she could live with Tony, since Vinny needed to be there for protection anyway. If Vinny and Tony could work it out between them, man to man, what did she have to lose? Other than maybe Lily never speaking to her again.

Sylvia and Tony decided to try it. They'd been waiting for Frankie's chat with Lily to take place. Neither had heard from Vinny yet. He was meeting them this morning so they were both nervous.

Sylvia silenced her phone. It was Lily calling again, and Sylvia wasn't ready to enter that lioness's den, not quite yet. Bear had texted the night before: SHE KNOWS. Sylvia sipped her six-adjective coffee and considered the gorgeous man across the tiny Starbucks table from her. The tiled patio was half-filled with patrons on computers and couples with dogs resting at their feet.

"Why can't you just be straight?" she asked Tony.

"If I were straight, I would have never pursued your hubby and, therefore, never met you."

"Actually, Tony, that does more to support my argument than yours," Sylvia said when she had worked through his logic.

Logical or not, she and Tony bonded over their mutual grief following Kyle's death. They shared memories of him nobody else knew...his hopes, dreams, desires. They visited places he would have loved, saw the world through his eyes. In time, they disclosed their own hopes, dreams and desires to each other. In the process of saying goodbye to Kyle, they became anchors for each other.

"Besides, if we were married you'd just run off and have an affair with Vinny."

"Well, yes. I would. But as I've told you time and again, that's the problem. I'm single. He's single. I want to jump aboard, but he won't do the deed until after the I do."

"I know. But my problem, dear Sylvia, is bigger than yours. You get to keep me as a friend, and Vinny as a husband-to-die-for. I get to head up a mob of weapon-wielding thugs I have no interest in ever meeting...dark alley or light of day."

"Yes. I see your point. But if we do this, the three of us, if we go meet the mob ancients in the old country...the results aren't bad." She made an air-list on her fingers. "You take care of your grandfather's wishes. He takes care of Lily. Frankie teaches you what you need to know. Vinny handles the actual execu...er, running of the day-to-day." She took a sip of her cooling drink. "Maybe the Sapienza family becomes known for good works under your leadership."

"Duck! Or was that a flying pig?"

"Okay, make fun. But it sounds good to me. Especially the part where Vinny and I..."

The phone distracted her as it vibrated around on the table like a furious lightning bug. Lily again. Sylvia sighed. "Do you ever get over the fear of disappointing your mother?"

Tony patted her hand. "She'll see the good parts of the deal when she calms down and knows how happy you are."

"She's going to hate that the deal was made without her knowledge."

Tony shrugged. "Better to ask forgiveness than permission, as they say."

"Actually, Lily is the one who taught me that. Unless it involves *her* permission, of course."

"Bear is pretty smooth. Maybe he's convinced her it's a good idea."

"Here comes that flying pig again."

"Um, don't look now but I think that's Vinny coming this way."

"Oh God, Frankie must have explained it all to him, too. Oh God!"

Tony and Sylvia stood at the same time. Vinny wound his way between the other patrons on the patio. As always, the very sight of him made Sylvia shiver with passion...maybe Tony shivered with fear. Would Vinny unload his considerable weaponry on them both?

The mobster stopped in front of her. The three encircled the tiny table. Dogs and coffee fanatics looked up. Tension built. High noon.

"You will do this?" Vinny's chiseled face was as deadpan as Mount Rushmore. "You will marry me now?" With no warning, he sank to one knee.

Sylvia felt heat from her core hit her face in an explosive blush. "Yes. Yes, I will."

As Vinny stood, he somehow picked her sturdy body off the ground and swung her in the air. One of her Michael Kors loafers took flight, landing two tables away.

Is he going to throw me?

Tony must have wondered the same thing. He moved forward. "Ah, Vinny..."

But as Vinny twirled her around, his dark eyes only flashed for her. A glorious smile spread across his face, a smile no one had ever seen before. Vinny lowered her to the ground as lightly as a floating feather. "You will be my wife!" Then he turned that high beam grin on Tony and bowed. "You, Antonio, will be my capo as your grandfather has been before you."

Tony retrieved her shoe, and Sylvia hopped on one foot, putting it on the other. Then Vinny insisted on the scariest part of the whole thing. "There is an act I must do," he said with a sigh, the huge smile dimming several hundred lumens. "I must ask *Signora* Lily for your hand."

Sylvia felt instant fear for her muscled newly intended. "I don't know, Vinny. Maybe we could just elope?"

"No, it must be proper."

Tony tried to help as they left the cafe. "Don't worry, Syl. Vinny held off the Pappalardo brothers singlehandedly. All three of them. Their sister, too. I think he can stand up to your mother."

Sylvia noticed a shrug of Vinny's magnificent shoulders as he murmured, "*Signora* Lily is a tough lady."

Tony said, "Think of it as your first test for me. If you can protect yourself and your soon-to-be bride from Lily, you are up to any protection I'll ever need." He turned one way, and the couple turned the other, to face a fate that might just be worse than death.

* * *

The gang was on the patio when the newly betrothed arrived, hand-in-hand. Bear, Charlie, Eunice, Jessica, Ben, Baby Benny, Good Fella, and Folly all slipped away, leaving the newcomers in the sole company of Lily. Even Furball had the good sense to lift his heavy self off a seat cushion and meander off to some other cat corner.

Lily felt the sudden departure as though a temperature drop cued a bird migration. She looked up from her roses, saw the approaching couple, set her pruning shears on the patio table, and took a seat. "No weaponry on me, Vinny. I'm harmless."

"I am here, *Signora*, to..."

"I know why you are here. I wish to speak with my daughter."

Vinny moved toward a chair as Sylvia stepped forward.

"Alone." Lily sounded snappish even to herself.

In a motion as fluid as a cat - one far thinner than Furball - Vinny righted himself, looked to Sylvia who nodded at him, and he, too, dissolved from the patio.

Sylvia sat next to her mother. "I am sorry if we hurt you," she began.

Lily held up an old hand. The skin was loose and the pale nails showed a trace of gardening dirt. Her fingers trembled just a bit. "You've all had your say with each other. Now I will have mine."

Sylvia complied. "Of course."

"I've wished renewed happiness for you, Sylvia. It's all I've ever wanted for you. I have been content as a widow, but it's a lonely path at times. Not the choice for everyone. I believe it's time for you to find love again.

"If I could choose the man for you, he would ideally not be a mobster. Somehow, I think any mother has the right to question a thing like that. But questioning is all I can do. I don't know what danger it may mean, or how many nights you will wonder whether he'll come home unharmed, or what ethical questions you might have to ask yourself as time goes on.

"But if you must choose a good fella, well then, Vinny is the best of them. He has done great things for me and for everyone else who lives here. He has honor and integrity. I will not oppose it. I wouldn't expect you to comply with my objection anyway. You make your own choices, and I am very proud of that." Lily stopped for a moment. "I only feel sad that nobody thought I could be consulted in advance."

"Would you have agreed? Really?"

"Sylvia, my love, I would have fought against it. Looked for another, safer path. But if it's what you want, I would have certainly backed you. Safety is never a given. None of us is ever safe. I don't count on it for myself, nor can I count on it for you."

"I don't know if it's the right thing, either, Mom. But I want to try."

"Then by all means, Syl, do it."

As they hugged, Lily said, "I'll tell you who really better not count on safety. Bear Jacobs, that's who. He'll get what's coming to him one of these days."

Sylvia laughed, and Lily called for Vinny who materialized as fast as he'd disappeared.

"Now, young man, ask your question," Lily said.

"I wish to marry your daughter," Vinny said, staring down into her eyes, as beseeching as Folly asking for a treat. Her answer could determine misery or joy for the rest of his life.

"I wish for the same thing," Lily said.

Sylvia, feigning gravity on this solemn occasion, said, "I do, too."

"Mamma mia!" Vinny nearly exploded. He reached down and gathered his soon-to-be mother-in-law in his arms and twirled her in the air. "*Mia suocera!*"

Sylvia beamed before saying, "Vinny, you really must stop tossing the Gilbert women in the air. We don't all like it."

He set her down then Lily yelled, "Get out here everybody, and congratulate the lucky couple. Latin's Ranch has a wedding to plan."

CHAPTER THREE

Case Notes
September 28, 11 a.m.

    When I think about it now, I have to say there was no particular reason why the wedding was at Latin's Ranch. Vinny or Sylvia might have considered other options. But I don't remember that there was ever a discussion about it.

    Latin's Ranch on a Sicilian night. What could be better? Or faster, for that matter, since Frankie was eager for his grandson to be on his way to the old country. With his 'wife' and bodyguard at his sides.

    Maybe they rushed it a little too much. Sylvia, interior decorator that she is, would probably have liked more planning time. But all things considered, well, at least it's over and nobody was hurt. Not seriously, anyway.

    Sylvia's honorary grandfather, Frankie, was mostly to blame. I suppose he figured this wedding would be his last big festa. *Whenever Syl wanted simple, he wanted extravagant. And being a don, he got it.*

    Regardless of the order Sylvia placed, Frankie made sure the supplier knew this was a wedding hosted by the Sapienza family. Sylvia's tasteful requests were ignored.

The florists went crazy. The day of the wedding, the whole darn ranch smelled like Hawaii...who knew plumeria was the flower of Sicily? Sylvia's bouquet was so huge it would have been more appropriate as a centerpiece for a table or casket. Exotic-scented trees in pots lined the entire driveway. Plumeria were braided into the manes of all the horses. Folly, Good Fella, and Furball helped each other chew off their floral collars, but the canaries' cage could have been an entry in the Rose Parade, at least until Big Italian Guy knocked it over when he tripped on a lemon.

The towering display of Italian lemons was lovely until Good Fella and Folly leaped into the middle of it. Lemons rolled everywhere, but you already know that: see aforementioned Big Italian Guy (more about him later).

Fortunately, Bear and I managed to shuffle amidst the lemons as we danced. That's right. Danced. Bear set his quad cane aside and took my hand, and I danced with this prosthetic leg. Bear held me tight enough that I couldn't lose my balance. A woman has to dance at her daughter's wedding, and I admit the movement to music thrilled me as it had when I was whole.

The old shamus knew I was happy. But I couldn't tell him such a thing. He leaned down to whisper into my ear, "You're going to get even, aren't you?"

"Oh my, yes," I whispered back.

"And I'll never know when it's coming, will I?"

"Oh my, no."

"You have a wicked streak."

"Oh my, yes."

He grinned and, I believe, the old fool drew me in a bit tighter.

The vino order was as overboard as the flowers. A few bottles of fine champagne would have pleased Sylvia and Tony. But gallons of proscesso tumbled in that fountain of sparkling Italian wine. Red wine was imported from a familia vineyard at the foot of Mount Etna. Who knew how much Charlie could drink? And serious hangovers are likely to knock the pleasant right out of Chrissie and Will during their next work shifts.

We'll have Mexi-Sicilian leftovers for three years. Neither Aurora nor Frankie could be talked out of anything so roasts, pastas and cannoli filled the kitchen, dining room, and spilled over onto the patio. Nobody pushes our cook and our don around: the hired caterers must have gone home with post traumatic stress disorder.

Eunice, calling herself the oldest bridesmaid of all time, swooped about in a sparkly chiffon cloud, and the mother-of-the-bride wore the sleeveless peplum blouse and tuxedo pants from our cruise last spring. Bear was Vinny's best man in a rented tux...I must say the two made a fine-looking display of manhood as they stood together beaming at Sylvia.

Sylvia did not have time or inclination for a traditional gown, so she opted for a deep green silk wrappy thing. I have no idea how it stayed up. I'm guessing she was more interested in how fast she could get it off on their wedding night than in how appropriate it was for a wedding day. But it was stunning, as was she with her auburn hair piled around the emerald necklace Tony gave her. It was a match for the emerald and diamond ring from Vinny. Green seems to be the color of good luck in Italy.

After the ceremony and feast, the three of them left together in the Caddy (decorated, you guessed it, with plumeria) driven by Big Italian Guy. I wonder if it was the first time Vinny was ever in the back seat of that car.

I also wonder where they spent the night before their morning flight to Italy. Surely all three were not together. Just as surely,

Sylvia is unlikely to tell me exactly what happened after Vinny unwrapped that green silk dress. Which is as it should be. But I hope it was spectacular. I do love a good romance.

Lily Gilbert, Happy assistant to PI Bear Jacobs

After the trio left for Sicily, Big Italian Guy stayed at Latin's Ranch. He was seen skulking around the house, the barn, along the fence line like a man with too little to do and nowhere to do it. He started joining the residents for meals.

The first time it happened, Frankie said, "With your permission, Jessica, Bear say I need assistant while Vinny es gone. Es Enzo."

"Of course, Frankie. Your friends are welcome here," she said pleasantly, although Bear could see those squinty lines appear at the corners of her eyes that meant her boiler was getting stoked.

Her husband Ben didn't seem to notice. "You're the guy that delivered the Husky pup to us, aren't you, Enzo?" he asked, passing a platter of vegetables roasted in oil, lemon, and garlic.

B.I.G. showed no inclination to answer but cut his eyes sideways to the don. Frankie said, "Es okay to speak, Enzo. These people are...*associates* of mine."

Great. Now we're all mobsters, Bear thought. *Jessica will love that.*

"Oh, Bear. Could I see you in my office after dinner?" Jessica said, maintaining that pleasant smile. "A small matter."

Crap.

B.I.G. chewed slowly, as though processing all this complex information. At last, he said to Ben, "Sì."

71

"Good pup, that Husky, although he still pees in the cat's bed," Charlie added.

Ben nodded. "Time something took Furball down a peg or two. Been king of the hill too long."

Meanwhile, Bear turned the highchair toward himself and commenced shoveling pureed carrots into Baby Benny's moving target of a mouth. Bear had a knack for getting veggies on the inside of the rollicking baby. It was a good time to remind Jessica what a helpful son of a gun he could be.

After dinner, everyone dispersed so the clean-up crew could settle the kitchen and dining room for the next day. "You. Come with me," Bear murmured to Lily.

"Why? You need back-up?"

"Might be."

"You're the one called on the carpet, not me."

"She likes you better than me."

"Everyone does."

"Do I have to do this alone? What kind of assistant are you?"

"I'll go. But it's curiosity on my part. Not any desire to help you."

Bear sighed. In an ass-kissing tone entirely unnatural to his normal repertoire, he said, "I'm obliged for the many things you do for me, Lily."

"Don't patronize me. I'm still mad at you."

They took chairs in front of Jessica's desk. Bear felt like a grade schooler, one awaiting a crack across the knuckles with a ruler.

Jessica opened fire. "What's going on, Bear? No misdirection now. Please tell me the truth. If anyone here is in danger, I can't allow it. You know that, right?"

He looked at Jessica's untamed curls, her freckles, her wide-eyed penetrating stare. He could not lie to this woman. Deceive maybe, but not lie. Jessica was a good soul, one who had kept his chestnuts out of the fire for ages. Sometimes, a guy just has to shoot straight. Now was that time. "Nobody wants to worry you, Jessica, least of all Frankie. He is well aware that his business could one day get in the way of yours. That day may have come."

"What are you saying, Bear? Is the baby in danger? Are you..."

She started to rise but he held up his hands. "Give me time to explain. No, we're not in danger. Here's the deal: The don is dying. He knows it. He wants a promise of peace for Latin's Ranch before he goes. And peace for Tony, too, as the new head of the family. So Frankie has set a meeting with two other gangs. It's a week from today. They'll want to hear what he has to say, so even if they do find out where he lives, they won't take any action."

"He's bringing mobsters here?"

"No, no. Both gangs have agreed. We're fine. The meet is elsewhere."

"Where?"

"Don't know. Don't care. But he's doing it there to ensure there's no danger to anyone here."

"If there's no danger, why is Enzo here?"

"Vinny wouldn't leave if the don didn't promise he'd have a new, oh let's call it valet, close at hand. Enzo can help you keep an eye on the old man, get him to the *medico* if necessary, drive him to and from the meet."

Jessica sat in thought, nibbling a cuticle. Her mouth trembled so slightly that only a trained observer like Bear would see it. He added, "And to be belt-and-suspenders safe, Frankie will move to Sam's trailer for the week, and Sam will sleep in the tack room. Enzo will take himself out to the trailer, too. So if there were even the littlest, tiniest bit of danger - which there isn't - it wouldn't be to anyone in the house."

"Frankie agreed to that?"

"Frankie suggested it."

Jessica appeared to be in deep thought again. Finally, she said with a break in her voice, "He's ready to leave us. Isn't he? I mean, to die. Frankie's pulling away from us."

Bear turned to Lily and glowered. She took the hint and said, "I think so, Jess. From what Eunice says, he doesn't want to wait out the last of the horrors of Parkinson's. He wants some control over the end. No extreme measures. No special nursing."

"A miracle could happen."

"Yes, it could, my dear girl. But you have to let Frankie define miracle for himself. At his age and with his diagnosis, his miracle might be an easy death. You'll have to talk with him about it, Jess."

Bear could see the caregiver struggle not to cry. Jessica was first and foremost a nurturer. To accept when a resident might choose death over life, well, that was crazy talk to her. But they all knew she respected them enough that she would bow to their wishes. "Then we will do our best to help him as long as he allows." She sighed and stood, pushing herself up with her hands on the chair arms. "Thank you for easing my concern about the danger of the situation, both of you."

She rounded the desk to hug her old friend, Lily. And for the first time, when she reached to pat the big man's hand, he grabbed her and enfolded her in a bear hug. "If this is inappropriate touching, I don't give a rat's ass," he said.

"Hug away, Bear," she answered. "Hug away."

* * *

Days passed at Latin's Ranch. By the fourth one, Lily was antsy.

Eunice spent most of her time in the trailer, where Frankie now resided. Latin's Ranch had used this cozy space before to hide people; Sam Hart, the barn manager, was a good sport about that. Sam and Jessica were installing a fence around the shed they now called Latin's Farm. The rescue burros had been moved there along with Gina Lola, who seemed to enjoy the role of godmother to the foundlings.

With Jess so busy, Lily wasn't getting gossip about the goings on between Cupcake and Doc McGrath. And she loved gossip almost as much as romance.

Romance brought her thoughts to Sylvia. She could have called Sylvia and maybe they would go out to lunch except, of course, Sylvia was out of the country. In Italy, the trio would be dining on antipasto. Or they'd be shopping for the world's finest leather bags and gloves, viewing art fit for the gods since, come to think of it, most of it featured the gods.

"Lily," said Bear.

"Wha...what?"

"You were about to spill that mug of tea."

"Oh dear. Thanks. Thinking about Syl."

"Let's take a ride."

"Can I drive?"

"No."

They clambered aboard Sitting Bull, their souped-up golf cart. It could muster 35 mph for short bursts. That was good enough to get them up the driveway, now denuded of potted plumeria trees, past the golds and reds of late autumn, and down the road to Reggie's Tavern.

"What are we doing here?" Lily asked.

"You looked like you could use something stronger than tea," Bear said.

Together they *kachunked* into the ancient rat hole.

"This is a rat hole."

"My kind of place," said Bear as they took a table or, more correctly, a slice of tree trunk on top of a barrel.

"Now what's got you down?" Bear asked, after they ordered a beer for him and a scotch for her.

Until that very moment, Lily hadn't realized she was down. But, the old detective knew his stuff.

"I shouldn't have ordered this rotgut if you want me to cry into my beer."

"This is the place for it. Everyone else does just that."

"I guess it's a bunch of things all at once. I'm too old to like change very much."

"Nothing to do with age. Nobody likes change, ever."

"Yeah. But maybe I'm feeling too old to accommodate it once again."

"Tell me."

"Maybe it's just the season to feel bittersweet, what with winter on its way. How many more do we have, Bear? But it's Frankie, too, and how his demise will affect Eunice. I'm worried for Sylvia, mostly. She's been through so much."

"She's a grown woman, Lily."

"I admit her letters sound just this side of delirious. But once a mother, always a mother."

"Well, I'm a constant. I don't change. I'm not going anywhere."

"Good to hear, Bear."

"'Course, I'm uncomfortable waiting for you to do whatever you're gonna do to me."

"Let me get this straight. You asked me along to listen to my tale of woe, thinking you could extract a promise from me to let you get away with hiding information you know concerned me. Is that right?"

"Yes, it is. You're very perceptive, Lily."

"And you think I should tell you what will happen?"

"Yes, I do."

Lily looked at the tired waitress in a grubby apron and a t-shirt that read *Take a Flying Duck* under the drawing of a famous animated quacker. "Miss," she called. "Could this gentleman have another beer or should he just go duck himself?"

* * *

Sami Bowles was a frequent flyer at the Six Waters Casino. She drank a little too much, bet a little too much, and was a flashy five-foot-six party on Jimmy Choo heels. She was a casino's dream, sweet-natured to one and all, plus a lure to male patrons as surely as salmon eggs are to trout. Drinking and betting in the vicinity of Sami was always a couple degrees hotter, so she was a guest who was protected. Otherwise, she could get herself in the damnedest problems.

Bear, Lily, and Charlie had met her one night at the casino, a Christmas or two ago. Bear and Lily had been following her on a case. Charlie was undercover as a delicate octogenarian which, in fact, he pretty much was. Sami was drawn to him, to support this old soul with her syrupy assistance. Charlie remembered her as one of life's missed opportunities; Sami remembered Charlie as an amiable geezer which, in fact, he pretty much was.

That's why her ears perked up all these months later, when she heard a gangsta-type mention the name Latin's Ranch. They were punks, probably teens just old enough to gamble. The one said to the other two that he was going there to off an old fuck, to make his bones for his bosses. Sami didn't really get it, but it sounded bad. Maybe he was talking about Charlie. So she rummaged in her oversized gold bag, finally pulling a cocktail napkin from the bottom where all the lint, gum wrappers, and sugar-free mints gathered. She held it up, straightened its bent edges, and sure enough, there was a number Charlie had written down. Charlie Barker at Latin's Ranch.

Sami went to the ladies room and placed a call.

* * *

Jessica and Ben were in Seattle on a rare dinner/show date so they were not at home when the phone rang around eleven.

Baby Benny was cradled in Bear's arms in the living room rocker, where they often spent time when they both had insomnia. Lily was on the sofa, enjoying emailed photos from Sylvia in Positano. The three musketeers were spending a few days there before heading to Palermo.

"Apparently all three enjoyed stomping on grapes following the harvest at a small vineyard," Lily said.

"Ugh," Bear replied, then added for Baby Benny's amusement, "Uggy poo-poo tootsie-wootsies." The baby squealed when Bear tickles his little big toes.

"Yeah. Syl is the queen of clean. Sticky feet by choice? Not sure I know my daughter anymore."

Chrissie was on duty so she answered the phone in the office.

"Charlie Barker?... Yes, he does live here...I'm sorry but he has retired for the evening...he seems fine..."

By now both Lily and Bear had perked up like a couple of meerkats. It was so quiet in the house this late that Chrissie's voice was loud and clear.

"Yes, I'm writing it down...you're Sami Bowles and you..."

Bear roared. "Chrissie, I'll take that."

"...ah, would you like to speak with his friend, Bear Jacobs?...Okay, I'll put him on...just a sec." Chrissie trotted in and exchanged the landline handset for a sleeping Baby Benny.

"Yo," said Bear.

"This is Sami Bowles. I met you..."

"I remember, Sami. Nice to hear from you. What can we do for you?"

She told the shamus what she had overheard.

"Did this gangsta kid say when?"

"No, but he sounded like jazzed, like working himself up, you know?"

Bear knew. "Sami, go take a quick peek. What are they doing now?"

"I can't tell you what they're doing, Bear. They're gone."

* * *

Bear rousted himself from the rocker, hollering, "Listen up!"

Lily set her laptop aside on the sofa cushion, and Chrissie rushed back into the room. Both were at the ready, troops assembling. Bear explained trouble might be driving their direction.

"Chrissie, go to the trailer and warn Enzo. Then get Sam's Winchester and come back here." Bear had reason to know that Chrissie was the best shot at Latin's Ranch, although not everyone shared in that realization.

"Is it serious, Bear?" was all the aide asked.

"As a missing heartbeat."

"I'm on my way."

"Lily, call Sam and ask him to pick me up. Call 911, too."

"Ah...maybe Cupcake, instead. She'll be faster with fewer questions."

"Good thinking." Bear and Lily both knew the deputy sheriff wouldn't doubt the urgency of a call from a bunch of dotty old people who thought something might or might not happen.

"Get Eunice out of the house. Charlie and Baby Benny, too. They'll be looking for the don in here. The trailer is safer." Bear headed for the door, *kachunking* at his personal best speed out to the porch and down the front steps. Within minutes, he heard Sam's truck growl into life. As it came down the long gravel lane from the barn toward the house, Bear saw Chrissie, lit by its headlights as she ran down the hill. Sam stopped for her, then skidded to a stop in front of the house. The long lean cowboy, in jeans, pajama top, and cowboy hat, leapt out of the driver seat as Chrissie slid down the passenger side. Bear saw the Winchester in her arms.

"Sam and I'll wait at the end of the drive. In case we can't reason with them, Chrissie, you take up position in the trees. For god sake, don't shoot to kill."

"We could use another gun, Bear," Sam said.

"Here's an extra from Enzo," Chrissie said, handing a shopping tote to Sam. "Brass knuckles and stilettos, too, in case you want to torture someone."

Bear grunted an approval. In the distance, he saw Sitting Bull. The lights glaring out of the trailer door were nearly blocked by the enormous form of Enzo meeting the golf cart.

Lily was taking care of the others, as requested. "Good girl," Bear said, although he'd never say such a patronizing thing directly to her.

* * *

It took Lily longer than she thought. She had to bang repeatedly on Charlie's bedpost with a metal serving tray. After she finally awakened him, she left him to transfer into

81

his wheelchair, then scurried as fast as a one-legged lady could go, down the hall to get her roomie. Eunice was awake, struggling into her coat-of-many-colors. "What's up, Lily?"

Lily didn't stop to explain. "Get Baby Benny then go to Sitting Bull fast. I'll push Charlie out then tell you all about it."

Charlie was in his wheelchair, an exhausting transfer for the old man on his own. Lily was relieved. "Good job, Charlie! Now we go." Tired or not, Charlie pushed the wheels himself, speeding along beside Lily. She was feeling the strain, too, but breathed deep to stay calm.

"What's going on? Is there danger? Are we safe?" Charlie whined as they dashed through the patio door.

"Sami Bowles called with a warning for you," Lily said.

"Sami? Sami Bowles? Called for me?" In an instant, Charlie shifted from fear to delight.

As they crept along the back of the house, Lily said with a big drip of sarcasm, "Yes for you. Proof she wants to jump your old bones."

"Well, she didn't mention *your* old bones. Or *Bear's* old bones." Charlie raked back his hair with a hand, apparently preening between pushes to his wheels.

Eunice was waiting for them where Sitting Bull stood charged and ready to rumble. She'd already placed Baby Benny in the cart.

Between them, the two women wedged Charlie into the back seat. He could lift with his arms by grabbing the cart's frame, but Lily and Eunice had to swing and haul his legs and butt.

"This kind of shit was easier when we were younger," Eunice said with a gasp.

"War may be hell, but so is old age," Lily muttered, patting Charlie's knee once he was situated.

"Sami Bowles is worried about *me*!" Charlie was in near-swoon.

Next, Eunice lifted the baby off the front seat and handed him to Charlie with a hushed hiss. "Stay calm. You have to be calm for Benny." Her cranky old voice then went quiet. The cranky young voice was still deep asleep.

Lily explained the situation to her passengers as she putted up the hill by starlight to the trailer. Chrissie had already alerted Frankie and his bodyguard. When the cart arrived, Enzo clambered down the trailer step to meet it.

"Take Charlie inside," Lily said. "I'll hold the baby while you do."

Enzo lifted Charlie from the golf cart, up the step, and deposited him on the trailer's banquette seat.

"Now Benny." Lily lifted the still-sleeping baby to Enzo. The kid looked no bigger than a beanie baby in those thuggish arms. But Enzo gently handed him back to Charlie.

"Thanks, Enzo," Lily said, sincerely relieved for his help. "We couldn't keep them safe without you."

B.I.G looked startled as though words of gratitude were a rare occurrence in the life of a mobster.

"Now you *Signora* Eunice," he said making a move toward the boss's little dove.

"Get away, you...you..."

"Enzo es a ewe ewe?"

"I'm staying with Lily." She clutched the frame of the cart.

"Eunice!" Frankie called from inside the trailer.

"I'm fine, my dear. But I want to help."

"I need her, Frankie. We'll be okay with Sam and Bear," Lily called to the don. Then to Eunice she muttered, "But first we go to the barn. I have a plan."

* * *

Minutes ticked past. Sam and Bear waited in the dark where the Latin's Ranch driveway met the county road. There was no traffic at this time of night, at least until a cruiser screeched to a halt next to the truck, its headlights nearly blinding them. Bear tensed then relaxed as he saw who exited the car.

"Wouldn't be a gun in that tote bag, would it, Sam?" asked Deputy Sheriff Josephine Keegan. Buttons on her plain clothes shirt were in the wrong holes as though she'd dressed in a hurry.

"No, ma'am. Just a ham sandwich. Case I get hungry."

"How about you Bear? Weaponry other than the blade inside your cane?"

So she wants to play sarcastic.

"Why's Doc McGraff with you, Cupcake?" Bear answered, believing that one smart ass deserved another. "No sick animals here, are there, Sam?"

"Not a one, Bear."

"Just out for a late night ride, are you, Doc?" Bear smirked.

The vet showed the good sense to say nothing.

"Okay, okay. What's going on?" Keegan asked.

Bear explained the situation, avoiding the mention of the mob as much as possible. Keegan and Frankie, cop and capo, were natural enemies so the less said, the better; they could coexist as long as they each turned the other cheek a long way away.

"Well, all seems quiet so far," Keegan said.

That's when *BEWHEAWHEAWHEAH* split the night.

It was only the beginning.

After one braying burro started the cacophony, a distressed howl layered on top. Then a second burro joined in with a double-barreled base, like foghorns harmonizing with each other. But it was the high strident wail that raised the arm hair on everyone in the driveway.

"Banshee?"

"Table saw?"

"Stripping gears?"

"No...Eunice!" Bear held his hands to his ears. "We better get down to the house."

Bear, Sam, Keegan and Doc scrambled into their vehicles and tore for the house. By then, they heard another shriek in the mix:

"OOO-OO-OOO! THIS IS THE SPIRIT OF SAPIEZAS PAST AND PRESENT. THOSE WHO WISH THEM HARM MUST FLEE...OR FACE A GHOSTLY FATE. OOO-OO-OOO!"

As the truck and cruiser pulled to a halt, three men bolted from the porch and dashed for the woods. Keegan took out after them on foot. Doc, looking bemused, followed her.

Bear had the presence of mind to cry, "Cupcake! Look out for Chrissie." Then, to add a little more terror to the gangstas' load, he added, "Lots of gunslingers out there packin' heat."

CHAPTER FOUR

Case Notes
October 2, 10 a.m.

After Eunice and I dropped Charlie and Baby Benny at the trailer, we'd gone to the barn to get Burrito and Concha, the two mini-burros. I figured we might need the noise they could make...Burrito had scared us plenty once in the night.

We knew the bad guys were young, maybe on their first foray. They'd probably be scared. And they weren't bright enough to keep their mouths shut, even in a casino.

Frightened and stupid. We could use that.

"They're probably city boys. Never heard a burro," I said to Eunice. "Might scare the stuffing out of them."

"I can ululate like a crazy person to add a dramatic touch," Eunice said. "I have very powerful lungs for a lady of some years."

"Great. And I'll be Ghost of Mobsters Past."

In the barn we tied two leads to the back of Sitting Bull and hooked them to the burros' halters. Slowly, I drove toward the house, the docile beasts trotting along behind. Things were going fine, until Good Fella galloped up and gave Burrito a playful tug on the tail.

Burrito didn't find it so playful. He kicked the pup then let loose that first blast before we were in position. Good Fella howled like an Alaskan werewolf (he seems unhurt, but he won't be practicing burro abuse again anytime soon).

I had planned to hide behind the house until the bad guys showed up, then release the racket. But once Burrito led off, the rest of us joined in. Concha made a din even worse than Burrito, and I had no idea how terrifying Eunice could sound once she really got to wailing. Since we were all in the spirit of the thing, I shouted out a threat about paranormal revenge.

Turns out the performance wasn't a dress rehearsal. The bad guys were already on the porch, having snuck through the woods. Maybe they didn't really think we were some cosmic force of the dead, but they must have figured we were crazy. They didn't stick around for an explanation. Heh!

Lily Gilbert, Tickled Assistant to PI Bear Jacobs

Bear was pissed. Well, mostly embarrassed, not that he'd admit it to anyone, especially that wiseass so-called assistant of his, Lily Gilbert. While he and Sam were stationed at the end of the driveway, armed to the teeth and ready for a rumble, Lily and Eunice had saved the day. With burros and a golf cart, for shit's sake.

Who knew the creeps would slink up on the house through the woods? Who would have thought mob wannabes would be such weenies? Surely they should have more swagger than that.

Chrissie caught them all as they exited the shrubs, with Cupcake right on their heels. The deputy arrested and hauled them away. Doc McGrath was on hand in case they needed any animal medicines. Bear figured the vet was the only one on the scene more useless than himself.

Since the young men actually accomplished nothing, there wouldn't be much of a charge. Probably they faced lectures from their own dons. The scratches from the blackberry whips might be the worst of it.

All this while Big Bad Bear and Six Shooter Sam stood around with their thumbs up their rumps.

Damn it all anyway, Bear had been outfoxed, outmaneuvered, and was now outraged. Maybe his days as a dick were over. Maybe it was time to hand in his roscoe, hang up his trench coat, and fade away into the misty fog. Maybe he'd seen too many noir movies.

If Lily wanted to get even, she'd found a damn good way. Even if she did deny it was part of a Play-Bear-For-A-Fool plot.

"You got me. I doff my detective hat to you," Bear said, wallowing in defeat.

"Bear, I didn't have time to think it through, you know," Lily answered. "You and Sam had the main route covered. Eunice and I merely took the backup route, you know, Plan B. We got lucky."

"So you weren't just getting even?"

"Not at all. I've been getting even all along by making you worry about me getting even."

"Run that past me again?"

"It was making you crazy, the *not* knowing. I wanted you to experience how it feels to be kept in the dark about things that involve you."

Crap.

He couldn't even stay very mad at her. She was making far too much sense.

* * *

The Mob Meet-Up was two days later. Frankie invited two other families, one of them headquartered south of the border, the other a far smaller but more efficient operation up in the Charlotte Islands. Both were drug-based cultures, which was business that Frankie deplored. His interests were more in the traditional rackets.

"They need not know the Sapienza family has no interest in their dirty enterprise anyway," the wily old don told Bear. "So I offer them to stay away from their business, in return for safe operation of our business."

"But if they're both involved with drugs, doesn't that just pit them against each other?" Bear asked.

Frankie smiled. "Exactly. Mobs lose when they turn on each other." Frankie's body may be crumbling but his brain was still intact.

Much to Bear's surprise, the crime capos didn't convene at a fancy hotel. They met at Reggie's Tavern, where a few extra bad asses was business as usual. Bear delivered the don and Enzo in Sitting Bull. But he wasn't allowed to stay in the bar beyond the opening few lines.

The usual funk of sweat and stale beer was upped with the odor of gun oil from all the assembled weaponry. An assortment of bodyguards lined the walls, failing to appear casual. Three dons huddled around a table made from a tree slab and a barrel.

They leaned in toward each other. Frankie began. "We are all dangerous men here. Each of us could have the other killed a dozen times over. It is wise then to meet in friendship, to trust that death is not convenient."

Way to go, Frankie, Bear thought. He was proud of the old man. Frail he may be, but a pretty smart *pizzelle* to the end. That's when Enzo tapped Bear on the shoulder and walked him out the door. The shamus nodded to B.I.G. and *kachunked* back to the cart, awaiting whatever came next.

* * *

It was a calm month before Frankie died. The gangs were peaceful, so maybe the Mob Meet-Up had accomplished its goal. The three travelers returned, and Tony spent many hours with Frankie before the old man died. Frankie had much to tell his grandson. And damned if the younger Sapieza didn't begin to take on the elegance and stature of the finest movie conmen of Lily's day...Sean Connery or Cary Grant or Frank Sinatra.

"I think more Clive Owen or Hugh Jackman," said Sylvia when her mother expressed this thought.

"You're too young to recognize the real thing," Lily answered. Then she saw the quiet glances that Sylvia gave Vinny, the knowing intelligence. Lily smiled. Her daughter knew the real thing, sure enough.

The only thing that kept the month from pure calm was the knowledge they all shared that Frankie was failing. That and the way Charlie behaved.

The old womanizer could not get over the fact that a hottie like Sami Bowles cared about him. He talked about it all the time. In fact, Bear finally told him to nip it. From then on, Charlie glowed in an aura of happiness...albeit a silent one.

Eunice and Jessica were with Frankie at the end. His little dove and his caregiver both loved him. Lily believed it was nobody's business what might have happened that last night, who might have helped whom toward a final goal. The pain was gone, and Frankie looked peaceful. So did her bestie, Eunice. It was all Lily needed to know. It was all anyone needed to know.

CLAN OF THE CRAFT BEAR

THREE BEARS

CLAN OF THE CRAFT BEAR

CHAPTER ONE

Case Notes
November 4, 11 am

"It's not a crap sale, Bear Jacobs. It's a CRAFT sale." The shooting stars in Eunice's ear lobes and around her wrist tumbled and sparkled as she crossed her arms and nodded her head for emphasis.

I've tried to tell her to ignore him, but he gets her goat whenever he wants. Speaking of goats, I have news on that front, too: in addition to the burros we have a couple pygmy goats. I'm told we'll soon have more based on simple biology. Latin's Farm is becoming too cute for words.

Anyhoo, about the craft sale. We promised Jessica we would help with the upkeep of our little group of rescue animals. Eunice came up with a strategy involving us all. Yes, even Frankie. Plans began just weeks before he died.

Eunice soldiered on after his demise, of course, because that's what Eunice does. She faces down grief, moves it to the side, and goes

95

on with the business of life. I alone hear her in the night, when tears overcome her. We don't need to speak, but she knows I am awake with her, keeping vigil in the dark.

Preparing for the craft show is a great distraction for us just when we all can use it. Of course, none of us knew then how serious the competition at craft fairs could become.

Or how deadly.

Lily Gilbert, Crafty Assistant to PI Bear Jacobs

Morning light streamed in the living room window, showering the residents gathered there. It felt like summer although it was early November. Eunice broke the silence with a rattle of the newspaper. "Good gracious! Electrocuted. Imagine that."

"Capital punishment somewhere?" Lily asked, looking up from her book. She removed her reading glasses and rubbed her nose. *Gotta get a better pair of specs.*

"Punishment, yes. Capital, no. A woodworker electrocuted himself with what they call fractal burning."

"Never heard of it," Bear said, looking up from Baby Benny who was happily drooling all over the big man's shirt. The ancient Hawaiian print could only be improved with puddles of baby spit.

"It's a way to etch a design into wood. Says here, you 'slowly apply high-voltage electrical current to a wood surface wiped with a conductive solution. Sparks move across the wood, creating a burn pattern on the surface.'"

"Sounds treacherous," Charlie said.

"Apparently it is." Eunice folded the paper to the page and handed it to Lily who looked at a picture of etched wood.

"It looks beautiful. Like trees blossoming." Lily next handed the paper to Charlie.

"Beautiful but deadly, apparently," Eunice replied. "If you touch the wet wood while the current is going through it, you can kill yourself. This guy did just that."

Bear asked, "This guy was a pro?"

Eunice said, "Well, I guess you could say that. He did terrific work. Wall hangings, tables, you name it."

"You knew him?" Charlie asked, handing the paper on to Bear. Benny commenced to drool on it, too.

"*Of* him. Hans Huffman. One of the leading artists in the state. He was a mainstay at art fairs. I'm sure he would have been at ACES. Imagine being offed by your craft."

"You mean like knitting needled in the eye?" Charlie started it. The rest of the Latin's Ranch gang couldn't help but join in.

"Gagged by lace hankie."

"Hanged by macramé."

"Chloroformed with crochet doilies."

"Poisoned with pens."

When they went back to their reading and baby-cooing, Lily thought about ACES. The Arts & Crafts Expo of Snohomish might just kill them all with everything Eunice expected them to do.

Eunice first introduced her plan about a month ago at breakfast. Charlie, Lily and Frankie had agreed to give it a go. But Bear hadn't so much as bothered with a "Let me think about it," or a "Sounds interesting." He'd gone right for, "Hell, no."

"Oh, come on, Bear. It'll be fun!" Eunice had insisted. She was not used to taking no for an answer.

Lily knew *this* Bear might be her BFF's nemesis. This was stubborn Bear. He'd pushed back from the table, slapped his napkin down next to an empty plate, and crossed his big arms over his bellyful of scrambled eggs. "I'd collect the money in a crafty way. But I'm not knitting doilies."

"That would be crochet," Charlie corrected.

"Whatever," Bear growled. "Not doin' it." He stuck out his lower lip.

So that's where Benny learned such behavior, Lily thought.

That was then. Now there was less than a week left for them to craft their hearts out. Eunice had long since rented space at the ACES exhibition hall and a booth that Ben promised to help them assemble for the days of the Expo. Booth signage was made, including a ten foot banner, naming the booth *Latin's Ranch Resident Round Up.*

Eunice planned that all the residents would create their favorite crafts, with proceeds going to Latin's Farm for abused domestic animals. She footed the bill for supplies, planning on payback from sales. They'd take turns in the booth, selling and demonstrating how productive oldsters can be.

Not a bad idea, Lily thought, *except Eunice is the only true crafter in the group.*

Lily and Charlie, to varying degrees, got to work. Lily knew Eunice was worried whether the rest could make enough variety to sell, especially now that Frankie wasn't there to help. Bear still hadn't budged.

"Okay, let's update," Eunice commanded.

Lily did not craft anymore, but she gardened, so she'd ordered supplies from a nursery and an online craft supply outlet. She was filling windowsill-sized rectangular pots with pygmy plants: ferns, succulents, evergreens, groundcovers. Each had pebbled paths with tiny benches or a windmill or family of bunnies to give it the look of a storybook locale. Forced by Eunice to come up with a name for her creations, Lily called them Lily-putian Landscapes.

"I have two dozen done and a dozen to go," Lily reported.

"And you, Charlie? You're helping Lily?"

"Well, yes. But I have a surprise of my own," Charlie's high-pitched voice warbled with delight. "Still working out the details. But I'll let you know soon. It's gonna be groovy, dude."

Groovy, dude?

"Come on, tell us, Charlie," Eunice urged.

"Nope, it's a surprise." He twisted an air-key to seal his lips. "Mi ips ar eeld."

"What's he up to Bear?"

"Don ell'em, Air!"

"No worries, Charlie."

"What about you, Eunice? Will you be ready?" Lily asked.

Eunice glowed with pleasure. "As you know, I'm creating a full line of accessories for mobility devices. I've decided to call it Cane Mutiny. There's simply no reason accessories for seniors have to be so darn dull."

Lily wondered what Eunice might define as dull, coming as she did from the antithesis of that world. As Eunice explained her product line, her boney arms flapped in a blouse with all the colors of macaw wings. Her spiked hair gleamed with a new application of orange. She lifted samples of her wares from a tote bag as she explained, "I have Spandex cane covers to match their owners' outfits, glitzy bags with Velcro tabs to attach to walker handles, and seat pillows for wheelchairs with hidden compartments for wallets and keys along the side edges."

"Plus a hollow for your privates," said Charlie who suffered sores in that sensitive area from sitting too long.

"Well, yes, at least in the pillows for men," Eunice replied. With a winsome intake of breath, she indicated a pillowcase's clattering fringe accessory and added, "Frankie helped paint all these tiny wooden hoops so I'd be ready." The mobster was gone, and Lily knew his little dove mourned his passing. The wooden hoops were a sweet memory for her of final hours spent together.

"Why didn't you ask me how I'm coming along?" Bear asked.

Eunice stopped. Then she frowned. Lily knew she'd been irritated with Bear since his refusal to take part. "Ask you what?"

"What I'm making for ACES?" He sent a text as he talked, his enormous hands obscuring the cell phone almost entirely.

"Well, Bear, you made it very clear that..."

"I'm not a complete ratbag, Eunice. I know when you're being a silly ninnyhammer versus when animals actually need our help."

"Really, Bear? Really?" Eunice looked like an orange poodle awaiting a treat, wiggling in uncontrollable excitement.

Bear paused. He knew a dramatic moment when he created one.

"So what are you doing, Bear?" Eunice looked close to explosion.

"Sam had a pile of barn wood too small for much else. So we're making birdhouses."

"Birdhouses!" The disappointment showed on Eunice's face and worked its way down her body as she slumped. "Well, that's a nice idea but I'm sure lots of other crafters at ACES..."

"Not like these. Hey, Sam!" he yelled toward the back door. "Hurry it up!"

The barn manager, presumably in answer to Bear's text, came in with birdhouses dangling from both hands.

Lily stared at them. "Why... those are Reggie's Tavern!"

"Correct. We're making birdhouses of the gin mills in town. Guaranteed to fly out the door, so to speak."

Lily didn't doubt it. They were damned adorable, complete with the weathered front door, beer ads on the windows, and the *Re gie's Ta ern* sign with its missing letters.

"Working up a model of the Irishman now. Might soak that one in whiskey. And Charlie, we can sure use your help. Of course, we may have to visit all the bars in town to be sure we get them right."

"Count me in!"

"Bear, what a fun idea! You really aren't such a jerk of all trades, after all," Eunice beamed.

* * *

Throughout the afternoon, Latin's Ranch was unusually quiet. Residents were busy with their digging, sawing, painting, and snipping. When the mail arrived, Jessica found Bear on the patio, checking the electrical connection to Sitting Bull's battery.

She handed him an envelope and said, "I had to think for a minute who Alvin Jacobs was. I never think of you as Alvin."

"Me either. Better name for a chipmunk," Bear answered, taking his letter from her as she went on her way to deliver a *Vanity Fair,* probably to Eunice. He looked at the envelope for a long time, then stuffed it into his shirt pocket.

Bear rarely got mail. He read *True Crime* online with a guilty pleasure similar to Lily and her romances. He received junk mail, but not much now that he was too old to interest any marketers but funeral homes and hearing aids.

He replaced Sitting Bull's front seat over the battery compartment. The battery wasn't lasting as long as it once did, it seemed to him, but the connections all looked fine. He brushed dust off his hands, rubbing them together, then lowered himself onto a deck chair with an audible *uuff.* The unseasonable warmth of the sun heated his shoulders and face, while a breeze tried to dry the sweat he'd worked up over the golf cart. A lemonade would go down easy, but he didn't want to ask an aide to get one, not when they were understaffed. Maybe a beer from Reggie's but no, he'd already bought two this week and money *was* an object. He really should get busy on another bird house. Charlie had painted lots of tiny beer signs, windows, and doors so Bear had plenty of pieces to assemble.

Crafts are crap, he thought with a sigh.

Instead of moving, he continued to sit, basking in the sun. Good Fella came and dropped a tennis ball at his feet. Bear ignored him. To get Bear's attention, the Husky dropped the ball *on* his foot. Bear leaned down, grabbed the toy, and heaved it as hard as he could throw, sending the dog into a joyful, yapping tizzy as he raced to beat it to the ground.

Bear pulled the envelope out of his pocket and looked at it again. The name on the return address was Jeff Jacobs. It was a name he hadn't heard in years. Jeff Jacobs was his brother's name.

* * *

Jessica knew the residents enjoyed company, and she often provided it in the form of guests around the Latin's Ranch dinner table. Deputy Sheriff Josephine Keegan and Doctor of Veterinary Medicine Bohannan McGrath were favorites, especially now that they appeared to be a couple.

Jo eagerly accepted an invitation for them both. She was no cook so her meals were often whatever she could grab at Burgermaster or Dick's. An actual meal prepared by Aurora, Latin's Ranch amazing cook, was heaven on a plate. On the formal Sicilian nights, Aurora and the old don, Frankie, used to create a variety of comfort food all their own, a fusion they called Mexi-Sicilian. But tonight, it was a Northwest Pacific autumn bonanza of sautéed wild salmon, roasted golden beets, a salad of fresh melons, feta and hazelnuts, and individual blueberry cobblers.

Holy kamoley.

She'd even dressed for the occasion. Her sheriff's uniform was drab. When not in uniform, she usually opted for earth tones. *Drab.* But tonight she wore a sleeveless dress in swirling colors, and the cutest sandals she had ever seen. They'd cost a mint and had far too little leather in their strappy construction to merit the price. She'd simply lost her head over her feet, even indulging in a pedicure. Jo's hair was no longer pulled back in a utilitarian, cop-like bun at the back of her neck. Tonight it was on the loose, flowing in rich dark waves.

She hadn't counted on that old bastard Bear looking at her and remarking, "Well, Keegan, tonight you *look* like a Cupcake. All cute and girly. Might as well be wearing sprinkles in your hair."

Eunice gasped. "Oh, what a fun idea!"

Lily shot a stink-eye across the table at Bear, and Keegan did, too. The others had the good sense not to snicker. Then Lily came to the cop's rescue. "What are you working on, Jo? Share with us what you can."

"Well, let's see. We've been keeping an eye on the homeless camp out near the county park."

"The one run by that woman, ah, Rita?" Lily asked.

"That's the one. No trouble yet, but the population keeps growing. She's tough, but I worry for her." Keegan had been undercover at that camp when she was kidnapped and nearly murdered. Rita the Tent Master had called in the help she needed. For a moment, Jo was rattled thinking about that dark time. Doc's hand touched her arm bringing her back to the present. Since it was Bear who had saved her, she decided to offer him a smile. The old curmudgeon did have redeeming qualities now and then.

"What about that artist?" Bear asked. "The fractal burn guy? Electrocution wasn't really a mistake on his part, was it?"

Jo stared at the old man. What a clever fellow he was. Or maybe just a cynic. Whatever, law enforcement had come to the same conclusion, but what did Bear have to go on? "Why do you ask?"

Bear scratched his chin under his beard. "Seems to me if the guy was a pro, you know made a living from it, he'd know how to avoid nuking himself. Besides, when a story doesn't have much follow up in the press, it's because law enforcement isn't revealing all they know."

Keegan nodded. "You're correct. At first, we assumed he touched the wood and completed the circuit of current. It was a deadly accident. Or maybe a suicide."

"But?"

"Judging by footprints in the sawdust in his studio, another person might have pushed him onto the wet plank while the current was live. The path of the current led right through his heart. Severe burns."

"Eww," Charlie and Eunice said in unison.

"And, I assume, someone must have been there to turn the current off?" Bear asked.

"Exactly. Somebody turned it off."

"Any motives?"

"Plenty. People we interviewed complimented his work but not him. Seems Hans Huffman was an unlikable man who felt free to tell you why he thought you were an idiot. Boozer and blowhard. Total believer in conspiracy theories."

"Like what?" This time Lily was the interrogator since Bear had stuffed his mouth with salmon.

"He swore the feds knew about 9/11 in advance, and that Princess Di was murdered, and that the moon landing wasn't real. Stuff like that. If there was a dark side, he believed it.

Thought people were out to get him." Keegan shrugged her shoulders.

"Huh," Bear swallowed, then spoke. "Maybe he was right. Maybe something he believed got him killed."

CHAPTER TWO

Case Notes
November 14, 9 pm

We made it! Our booth at the Arts & Crafts Expo of Snohomish was ready when ACES opened for business today. Our 10 x 20 foot space is doublewide and looks damn inviting. Whatever Eunice does, she does well.

This show attracts crafters from all over the Northwest, being so close to the holiday season. The vendor parking area was astounding. We saw enormous rigs there, motorhomes, fancy RVs with storage trailers. I had no idea the craft show circuit had so many vendors who must make a decent living as they travel show to show.

Based on that parking lot - and the average age of the vendors - I'd say that crafters are kind of the new carnies. Older people traveling the country, showing two or three days a week, living the rest of the time in comfy rigs. Not a bad retirement if you have the talent, strength and the health to do it.

A lot of these guys know each other. The camaraderie seems pleasant enough, but not all of it is fun-and-games. I've already seen infighting about whose location is better, who took an inch too much, who shouldn't offer free fudge samples if the cheese and sausage crew next door isn't allowed to do the same. The same kind of squabbling you'd expect from a flock of free-range chickens, each aiming for the best worm.

Interspersed among the big boys are folks like us, local artisans hoping to make a buck or flogging for a charity. Some are selling things that are, well, dreadful. Hard to imagine why anyone would want them. But many are great. Barn's Bowls has seriously gorgeous wooden artistry; Hanging Beach mobiles are masterpieces of driftwood, shells, and beads; Raggedy Rugs uses recycled t-shirts to create delightful designs; the berry bowls at Art of Pottery are wonderful, and yes, the guy's name is Art.

Latin's Ranch Resident Round-Up opened with all our crafts, plus Charlie, Eunice and me to sell them. Bear, Ben and Chrissie will take turns, too. Yes, I did say Chrissie. Our favorite aide. Somehow she found the time to crochet a line of baby clothes she calls Glad Rags for Busy Moms. The baby sweaters don't have button holes...they have easy loops. Same for pants that go over diapers. Practical stuff. Smart. Like Chrissie.

Frankie was supposed to be handling back stock from home as we need it. Sam and Ben stepped up to do that for us. We are blessed that way.

The bar bird houses are hanging at one end, attracting no small amount of comments and brisk sales. Next are my little gardens; Charlie built me a display that looks like window sills. Eunice's Cane Mutiny accessories take center stage where the booth has most room for wheels and walkers and other mobility-equipped shoppers to gather around. Charlie is at the far end with the product he just revealed this morning.

Turns out, after Aurora leaves for the evening, Charlie has been using her kitchen. He developed a 'secret' recipe for cannabis butter that he swears has all hallucinogenic effects removed, leaving nothing *but pain relief. He's selling cookies he calls Grandpa's Little Helpers. Jessica will be appalled when she finds out. But he's likely to be busted before she does. Weed is legal in Washington, sure, but I doubt Charlie has read all the rules.*

Lily Gilbert, Mover-shaker Assistant to PI Bear Jacobs

The crowd came in with the action of ocean waves. They hit the show in massive forces, then ebbed before washing over the vendors once again. During lulls between buyers, the sellers could get out to see what else was on the floor, a good way to gather new ideas for their own displays. Lily and Eunice were happy in their space, but Charlie and Bear took a break in the action to walk the show.

"This place is a babe magnet," Charlie said with delight, swiveling his head left to right, flashing a lupine grin. "Maybe I'll create a line of products called Babe Magnets. Pictures of kittens and chocolate cakes and shoes and Idris Elba. That'll attract 'em right to me."

Bear looked around. He saw many women of all sizes, ages and dress codes. No more and no fewer than in most weekend crowds. Maybe Charlie wasn't getting out often enough. But, Bear had to concede, he might actually sell more babe magnets than weed cookies.

The exhibition hall had what passed for a cafe at one end, offering coffee, soda pop, pre-packaged Danish and sandwiches of unknown origin. As they made their way to that end of the circuit, Bear said to Charlie, "You go on around, then back to the booth. Think I'll stop here for coffee."

Charlie saluted then pushed himself on his way. He used his wheelchair to part crowds or to meet people. His strategy was that a gal found it hard to ignore a mild-looker geezer using a mobility device to cut into her territorial imperative.

The shamus turned from Charlie and scanned the crowd in the cafe. He hadn't wanted to meet this guy at Latin's Ranch. Too personal. So they'd set an appointment here. The man was not hard to pick out, looking a lot like Bear's dad in the one dog-eared photo Bear had of him. He nearly overpowered the folding chair at the small round table.

Bear stood as tall as he could on his quad cane, sucked in his gut, and *kachunked* to the table. "Jeff," he said. "I'm Al Jacobs. People call me Bear."

The man stood to shake hands. He had dark, piercing eyes. Like Bear. He was tall, round-shoulder, well-muscled. Like Bear had been.

"So do I call you Uncle Al? Or Uncle Bear?"

* * *

When a vendor needed to use the facilities, ACES provided volunteers to keep an eye on the booth, although Latin's Ranch had enough people to cover their own. In the loading and storage area of the hall, there were restrooms just for show workers which were closer and faster for them than the public restrooms.

Lily was in a stall. Around her, toilets flushed, and she could hear running water at the sinks, soap dispensers being hammered, towel dispensers rattling. She was eavesdropping, an activity she loved almost as much as a morsel of good gossip. The two often went hand-in-hand. Her ears, still sharp as a youngster's, were a valuable asset for the assistant to a private investigator.

She was listening in on gossip right now. There were three women's voices at the sinks. Lily didn't recognize their owners, but she could keep them apart by their tones.

Alto was saying, "...he was such a shit. Wouldn't be surprised to find out someone helped him on his sorry-ass way."

Whiney asked, "You mean someone here? A crafter?"

Alto replied, "I dunno. But he was always bitchin' at one of us about some damn thing. We took too much space, we made too much noise, our work was no good. Asshole."

Raspy spoke up. "I agree. Huffman was a dreadful man, not that I would speak poorly of the dead."

Lily needed to see the speakers so she could identify them when she told Bear. He'd find something in this to help Keegan with her investigation, whether Jo wanted his help or not. Lily stood to pull up her undies and slacks.

Alto said, "We didn't like him, but nobody would screw with his equipment or push him into a current - *kill* him."

Raspy disagreed. "I wouldn't be too sure. You heard Patty talk about him?"

Alto asked, "Patty?"

Raspy answered, "You know. In a Lather about Leather. It seems he was in a lather about Patty, too, until he got what he wanted and dumped her."

Whiney said, "Or what's his name at the Iron Man booth. Remember, the two of them got into a brawl last year? Had to be separated by the Bee My Sweet Honey guy and a couple willing customers."

Lily hurried, always a mistake when you wear a prosthesis. As she yanked, her slacks caught on her artificial leg, a pinch of fabric in the bend of the knee. She began to wrestle with the tangle but her own weight locked it in.

Shit. Hell. Damn. Were her undies caught in there, too?

Raspy said, "I know some of the vendors think he pulled dirty tricks on them. Loosening bolts in their displays over night, blocking electrical plugs, stuff like that. Couldn't prove it, though. Probably just convenient to blame one source for all problems."

Lily had to hurry. She could hear the towel dispenser and knew the women would soon leave. With her pants still trapped in the bend of the knee, she grabbed the top of the stall door, threw the lock, and gave a push.

Lily realized that what the trio next saw was an old woman swinging on the top of a bathroom stall door, hopping on one foot while the pant leg on the other limb swung in the breeze.

Alto, Whiney and Raspy froze like deer in headlights. Lily clicked a mental photo; she'd recognize any of them again.

"Oh, hello ladies," she said, trying to sound jolly. "Don't mind me. This stretching is the perfect exercise for a one-legged vendor. Loosens me right up. Doctor's orders."

"Oh...I see...well, okay then." The three vendors said in unison as they lifted their eyebrows, swallowed their laughter and hustled out of the restroom. Lily, now with time to spare, straightened herself out, then hurried back to Latin's Ranch Resident Round-Up. But Bear wasn't there.

Where's a detective when you need one?

Lily continued around the loop until she saw the big man in the cafe with another big man who looked like a younger version of the older one.

What the hell? Bear has family? He never told me!

By the time she chugged to the cafe, Lily was pooped. She puffed up to the little table, pulled out the last folding chair, and plopped down, gasping, "Phewww! Hiya, Bear."

Charlie came in for a landing right behind Lily, wheeling himself to the tiny table. "Place is teeming with crafty foxes and artsy chicks!"

"Uh, is anyone actually minding the Latin's Ranch booth?" Bear asked.

"Oh sure. Eunice is there. Chrissie, too. Both of them better at the sales pitches than I am. And certainly better than you are, Bear," Charlie said.

"Oh come on. I only told one customer to pound sand."

"So who's your young friend?" Lily asked, grinning at the forty-something image of yester-Bear.

The guy flashed a smile so bright it nearly knocked her out of her seat. Skin around his eyes crinkled in good humor, and nothing about him seemed judgmental. She didn't sense disapproval or discomfort with her age or lameness; his super power was to open up and draw her in. "I'm Bear's nephew, Jeff. You must be Lily. And Charlie. We've just been talking about you. What a pleasure to meet you both. Wow! A real private investigator and two of his operatives."

Maybe Jeff looked like yester-Bear, but Lily was doubtful that Bear had ever been this open in his own youth. Bear's past was his own business, and he kept it to himself, but she often wondered what happened in his life that beat him into such cynicism. The people he trusted, laughed with, enjoyed were a very small population. Latin's Ranch and a few outsiders like Keegan, Sam and Doc. Otherwise, he mostly closed down around others, like a bear in hibernation.

She looked at him now and saw with surprise that he was at ease with this young stranger who was laughing with Charlie over Grandpa's Little Helpers. Bear had never mentioned Jeff to Lily. They couldn't be that close. Was he responding in joy to biological family? Lily felt a tug of jealousy.

"I've just told Bear about where I live," Jeff said. "My wife and I have a home near the ocean, out by Hoquiam. Our kids live in the area, and they have kids. They're Bear's great and great-great nephews and nieces. We'd love to have the patriarch of our family move closer to us."

Lily nearly wet her recently-straightened pants. Bear? Move from Latin's Ranch to live with family so far away? Would he leave her?

* * *

Jeff soon left, saying he would be back tomorrow for a quick visit before heading home. Charlie wheeled away to check on his cookie inventory. Lily turned to face Bear square on.

"Tell me," she said, knowing he would understand exactly what she meant.

He heaved an ursine sigh. "I've never talked about my family much. Didn't know I still had one."

"It appears you do."

Lily could see by Bear's face that his internal barometer was falling: delight in his nephew was morphing to sadness. "This Jeff is my brother's son. Same name. But brother Jeff and I parted ways decades ago. I went to Nam. He went to Canada. Never heard from him again."

"Of all the things you've investigated, you never investigated that?" Lily felt her brows crawling up her forehead as her eyes widened in disbelief.

"Lily, it tore my parents apart. They fought about it. Split up, even. Ma wanted him back, Dad wanted no part of him. They both were angry with me since I wouldn't take sides."

"Well, that's not fair," Lily sniped, indignant for her friend.

"Those were hard days with shitty choices for young people to make. Not my nature to criticize their decisions."

Lily's husband had died in that war, and both she and Sylvia had been discarded by his parents. She was well aware of the impact on family. Still, she questioned the split in Bear's. "But he just disappeared from your life?"

Bear gave the smallest of nods. "I always figured it was up to him to reunite. His choice. Maybe he thought I'd be ashamed of him. Maybe he was ashamed of me. Don't know. Never will. Nephew Jeff says he died a few years back, still in Canada."

"And Jeff found you."

"Fulfilling a promise to his dad to find me. Guess my brother didn't want me around, but he wanted his son to have family, and I'm all that's left. Nephew Jeff put it off for a while, but then moved his wife and kids from Canada to Hoquiam, following an office job with the logging industry. After that, he started looking for me."

Lily had so many questions, her tongue twisted around the batch of them. Before she could get one out, Bear said, "Not sure I want to talk more about it here, Lily. In public. In all this noise."

She relented. Her fear that he would leave Latin's Ranch had to shuffle aside until the time was right. "I agree. We'll talk about it later. In the meantime, I have a field report to debrief."

Bear faced her with relief. "Regarding?"

"The murder of the master crafter."

"Ah. Cupcake's case."

"Yes. And now ours, as well, I think." She told him what she had heard in the ladies room, the tale told by the three artisans about Hans Huffman. "Sounds like there might be motives for murder right here at ACES. A woman scorned, an artist demeaned, a crafter beaten..."

Bear harrumphed. "Well done. Most worthy of note." He patted himself down, found his phone in a pants pocket, punched in a number and left a message. "Cupcake. Come to Latin's Ranch this evening. We have information."

"You know, Bear, Keegan may have other plans. She can't always be at your beck and call."

"What could possibly be more important than us?"

* * *

"What's so important, Bear, that you feel free to order around the Washington State Sheriffs' Association?" It was well after dinner when Keegan arrived, but Aurora still provided coffee alongside sliced mangos over pound cake squares, drizzled with cinnamon crema.

"Well, not the whole association. Just you. The fact that you brought along Orwell is entirely your concern."

Deputy Detective Brandon Orwell was Jo Keegan's latest partner. At the moment he was trying to finish his dessert while keeping a soggy tennis ball out of his lap where Good Fella, the Husky pup, was determined it should be buried. Orwell had always been uneasy at Latin's Ranch, and the color in his ruddy cheeks did nothing to hide his nerves. He'd once made it clear to Lily - who'd told Bear - that he didn't believe it was proper for real sheriffs to consult retired private investigators with old lady assistants. But whatever his partner said, went. "Jo has him thoroughly buffaloed," Lily said.

Bear knew it. If he were inclined to care about such things, he'd worry for the young man. The kid had smarts enough to be a cop, but maybe not the personality. 'Confident' would not be in the top twenty descriptors of the lad. Bear thought about the criminals he'd faced in his life. Orwell would be so easily fooled or overpowered by them. He wasn't exactly hopeless, but he needed to be seasoned, toughened up. The old shamus wanted a stronger partner for Keegan, one more protective of her.

Keegan's last partner had been perfect until he'd let her down in no uncertain terms. Endangered her. Shattered her trust. Oh well. Maybe she needed a guy like Orwell now. One she could push around. Teach the skills he needed to do the job. Bear didn't know about all the crazy things women had in their heads. But he did know enough not to voice his opinion on this particular situation. If Keegan liked Orwell, then Bear had to accept he was a good kid. Might even help the kid along himself if the opportunity arose.

"Lily, please report what you heard to Detective Keegan. And to Detective Orwell." Bear let his assistant download all she'd heard while swinging on a bathroom door. She downplayed that part of it.

By the time Lily finished, Keegan was pulling on her lower lip while the WTF lines between her brows deepened in concentration. "Sounds like we better round up the crafters for more in-depth interviews," Keegan said. "Someone knows something."

"That's where we can help you," Bear said. "We're already on the scene. Undercover-like. We appear to belong at the craft show because we actually do. Let us ask around before you cops wade in and muddy the water with your flat feet."

Orwell ventured a censure. "Now, sir. Mr. Jacobs. That is no way to speak to Detective Keegan. Her feet are not muddy. I mean the waters will stay plenty clear. I mean..."

"Enough, Orwell. He knows what you mean. And he makes sense. But if he ever calls me Cupcake in front of you, you have my permission to employ police brutality on the old son of a bitch."

"It would be my pleasure, ma'am. Ow!" He plucked the tennis ball out of his crotch one more time.

CHAPTER THREE

Case Notes
November 15, 2 pm

Sad news to report. Another murder happened last night, this time right on the craft fair floor, probably about the time Keegan and Orwell were with Bear and me. The body wasn't found until vendors arrived to open their booths, early this morning.

I didn't see the body, but those who did say Raspy was found with one of her own felted scarves wrapped so tight around her neck that she suffocated. I'm glad I didn't have to view the ugly effects caused by an interruption of the brain's blood supply...the blood trickle from her ears, the crushed windpipe. I have too many nightmares of that already from the death of our dear aide, Alita. But that's another story.

Local police cordoned off the area. Since this is not a sheriff department investigation, Keegan isn't involved, not officially anyway. With separate jurisdiction, Huffman and Raspy appear to be separate crimes. No reason for the boys in blue to put the two together so soon. But Bear saw the connection and reported to Keegan.

Last night, Bear and I divied up who'd-do-what today. I headed out to search for Alto and Whiney since I didn't know which booths they womanned. I wanted to find out if they had any gossip to add, now that Raspy, whose real name is Cora Stanfield, is no more. Bear headed toward In a Lather about Leather. Charlie and Eunice stayed in the Latin's Ranch booth although foot traffic was low. Arts and Crafts shows aren't supposed to be dangerous so lots of customers left once they discovered what had happened, replaced with Lookie-Lous who arrived once they discovered what had happened. Lookers aren't buyers.

It wasn't a good morning for our happy gardens, birdhouses, cane covers and cookies.

Lily Gilbert, Saleless Assistant to PI Bear Jacobs

Bear carried two cups of coffee on a cardboard tray from the ACES cafe. He added a couple Grandpa's Little Helpers to the open cup holders. With sustenance in one hand and his quad cane in the other, he *kachunked* away from the crowd gathered around the dead woman's booth, making his way to the leather goods lady at the other end of the hall. He was on the hunt, and nearly unaware he hummed *The Third Man Theme*.

In a Lather about Leather had an extraordinary collection of purses, belts and bags. Even to Bear's eye, the abstract patterns on the leather were washes of glorious color. The woman who sold them wore one of her own vests, a vivid burst to brighten the plain wheat linen dress she wore beneath it. Bear pegged her as the young side of forty, but not by much. Maybe she'd been dumped by a heartbreaker, but in Bear's assessment this was a woman who had no doubt broken a few hearts herself. She sat alone in the booth, perched on a tall wooden stool, watching him approach. Her legs were crossed, and her foot slowly circled like the tip of a cat's tail when a specimen of interest comes near: in this case, Bear.

"If you're Patty, I've brought you coffee. And weed cookies. Caffeine and CBD may work together or against each other. I don't know. But if your mood needs altering, this should do it."

"Thanks, stranger. I'm Patty, but I think I'll pass on the provisions. Who the hell are you, and why does my mood concern you?" Her voice was a monotone, showing no surprise that a strange man might offer her treats.

This was not a woman to waste time with chit chat or to mince words. Bear liked her immediately and got right to business. "I understand Hans Huffman did you dirt."

"Dirty as a pig sty. What's it to you?"

"I'm a private investigator, helping with inquiries into his death."

"A PI with what appears to be a whole lot of miles on his carcass?"

"Travel is good for the brain."

"You have some ID?"

"Nope. Name's Bear."

"Well, I guess no imposter would choose a bear as a disguise."

"No. It is unlikely."

"Maybe I'll take the coffee after all. You can keep the cookies." She tapped the leg of an empty stool with her foot. "Have a seat. We talk until customers show up. Then you scram. Deal?"

"Deal."

"Am I a suspect in the murder of the nutjob?"

"Did you do it?"

"Wish I had thought of it. But no. I didn't."

"Then I don't suspect you. Can't speak for the official investigators. Tell me about him."

Patty confirmed what Bear already knew: Hans Huffman was not a likable man. But Patty had taken him on as a matter of interest, sort of a challenge. She was curious how a person could become such a conspiracy theorist.

"I admired him as an artist, and sometimes artists take a little extra effort to understand. I worked at knowing him. What I didn't expect was to fall for the dirtbag. Then, after I believed we were close, he up and told me to get lost. 'Don't want anybody knowing so much about me. You must be after something.' That's what he said. End of story."

Bear harrumphed and thought for a moment. "So you were caught in his conspiracy craziness?"

"Sure was. Just another liar not to be believed. Still, I think about it. How anyone can buy that everything is a scheme or a plot, be anti-vaccine, antisocial, assume all news is fake news." She shook her head. "What a sad way to live."

"Apparently somebody else found it more than sad."

"Sorry?"

"Somebody found it an unforgivable way to live."

"So you're assuming one of his conspiracy theories was the reason for his demise?"

"It's a place to begin."

"Really, I can't imagine that. I mean, his erratic beliefs didn't really hurt anyone but himself, did they? The moon landing a hoax? Big Foot is real? How is that shit harmful to your fellow man?" She cocked her head as if to reconsider, then she shrugged. "Of course, he hurt me. Guess that brings us back to Patty as a suspect."

Bear struggled off the stool and steadied himself on his cane. "I'm thinking you're far from the lead contender on that list."

"Thanks for that. And Bear? Would you leave those cookies with me, after all?"

Bear left, *kachunking* back to the Latin's Ranch booth with murder on his mind, but customer traffic had picked up. He had to vend. He sold a Reggie's Tavern birdhouse to Reggie. Two off-duty cops purchased The Irishman houses, and a woman commissioned Bear to do a bird bar from a photo of a haunt of her youth. Maybe BirdBars was a name he should trademark. Maybe Charlie, Sam and he could go into business, go national. Maybe...

Lily interrupted his thoughts, bringing him back to murder. "I talked with Alto. She says that Raspy, aka Cora, left her a message last night. Excited. Said 'Wait 'til I tell you what I just heard! I'm...' Then Alto heard some gasps and guttural sounds and lost the connection."

"Or the connection was strangled to death."

"My thoughts exactly."

"Lily, you have your computer here? Something I want to look up."

As Bear tapped the keyboard with oversized fingers well-suited for mistakes, Lily sold three Lily-putian Landscapes and two of Chrissie's Glad Rag baby tops. Eunice was pleased to see two women, both customers from the day before, pass by with her flashy cane covers already in use.

"Save the burros! Save the goats!" Eunice yelled, her hand fisted in the air. "Latin's Farm is their salvation!"

Meanwhile, Bear placed a call to Keegan.

* * *

In the late afternoon, Lily saw Bear with his nephew, Jeff. They were in the cafe again, but this time Jessica and Baby Benny were with them.

*That's odd. When did Jess find time to come to ACES? Why didn't she tell me? But no...*as Lily neared them, she saw that the young woman was actually a stranger and so was the baby who was cuddling and cooing in Bear's big arms. He was laughing.

Lily turned away, feeling instant distress on behalf of Baby Benny. How could Bear be so...so...*happy* with another baby? Then she realized he could be as damn happy as he wished, because this must be one of his own great-great-nieces. And the mother a great-niece, maybe a daughter of Jeff. The family was bringing in the heavy guns to steal Bear away. Move him from Latin's Ranch to somewhere out in Hoquiam which wasn't exactly the easiest part of the state to reach.

And, of course, that is what they should do. He should have the love and respect he never knew was available to him. She thought how lonely she would have been without Sylvia in her life. Bear would be right to move closer to his kin. He would.

She marched to the back of the hall, entered the restroom, went into the familiar bathroom stall and cried.

* * *

That night, Keegan stopped by again. This time she was with Doc, not Orwell. Eunice was excited to tell the vet all about the fair and the proceeds that would be coming in for Latin's Ranch. "I think we covered all costs by the end of today, and tomorrow we begin in the black. With a whole day to earn a profit, we should..."

Meanwhile, Keegan took Bear and Lily aside. "I want to thank you for the tip, Bear. How'd you tumble to it?"

"Something that Patty, the leather goods maker, said. We've been looking for a motive to kill a conspiracy theorist. But mostly, a person's crazy beliefs may irritate others, but don't actually hurt them. To find a motive, we need a belief that can actually be harmful ... or conspiracies aren't the motive."

"But so far, it's the only thing we've got to go on," Keegan said. "Other than being a known blowhard, he has little to set him apart."

"In passing, Patty mentioned anti-vaccine. Now there's a strange group of bedfellows. Some have religious objections. Others think the risk of allergic reactions is too high. Big pharma wants to sell them useless products. The diseases are near extinct anyway. Whatever the reason, an anti-vaxxer doesn't protect his kid."

"A motive starts to appear."

"Maybe so. Got me to thinking about an article I read a while back. I read it again today on Lily's computer. Research is showing that a high percentage of anti-vaxxers are also conspiracy nuts. If they believe that Diana was murdered or a magic bullet got Kennedy, well that isn't likely to hurt the guy on the next bar stool. But if they believe they shouldn't vaccinate their children, that's another story. Those kids could be seriously damaged. Not only that, a kid spreading disease can be a killer for another kid whose immune system is compromised or for an unprotected senior. Death isn't out of the question."

"It's a stretch, Bear. Kill someone because his kid endangers yours?"

"Not really a stretch, Keegan. Think of it this way. If an anti-vaxxer led to Baby Benny's death, I know a ranch full of people who'd be out for the parent's blood."

"So the motive for Huffman's death may be vengeance."

"That's what I'd be looking for if I were a big time deputy sheriff."

"That moves Patty lower on the hot seat."

"It does."

"Starting tomorrow, the big time deputy sheriff should start looking for a person whose loved-one was hurt by an anti-vaxxer."

"Or a teacher of an unvaccinated kid who was exposed. Or a drug salesman who wants to stop the spread of the anti-vax beliefs."

"I get the idea."

"Of course, it might still be something altogether different. Maybe an alien really is among us and targeted Huffman. Maybe neighborhood watch feared the stockpile of guns in his basement."

"There was no stockpile of guns in his basement."

"Gosh, I guess that's not it then."

"Okay. You've made your insufferably rude, grouchy point."

"Then my job here is done. And it's past my bedtime."

* * *

The next day was the third and last one of the ACES exhibition. Mid-morning, Bear watched as the Iron Man - Alan Medlar, creator of scrap metal wall hangings - was escorted out by a couple of cops. Keegan must have dropped a hint to the local guys. Rumors spread through the vendors like dysentery through a bus tour.

Lily reminded Bear of her conversation with Alto, Whiney and Raspy. "Iron Man was the guy who had a fistfight with Huffman. And his booth is right next to Cora's so maybe she overheard him talking about getting even with the woodworker. Maybe he was indiscreet."

Bear wondered if Medlar had a kid, one who might have become sick with a preventable disease. He assumed Keegan would be looking into that. If Iron Man had a kid die due to the Huffman's failure to vaccinate, well, Bear wouldn't be all that hasty to put the guy away. Except, of course, the murder of Raspy was an act with no forgiveness.

An angry Iron Man returned to his booth in the afternoon. He packed up and left the show, without a word to anyone.

"What's he doing here?" Charlie asked, picking up one of Eunice's display canes. It sparkled as he added, "Did he break out of the big house? Should we prepare to defend ourselves?"

"Charlie, put the weapon down," Bear said. "They probably don't have the evidence to hold him. But they'll be working on it."

Shortly after that, Keegan called Bear. "Pretty sure he took out Huffman. Details to confirm, alibis to trace. But he looks guilty to me. As for the suffocated woman at the show? That's up to the local cops for now. Investigations continue. But the deaths are connected. That seems clear."

* * *

That night, everyone at Latin's Ranch was tired, including Jessica and Ben. They had taken on the lion's share of breaking down the booth and packing up what few goods remained. Latin's Ranch Resident Round Up had been a hit. The ACES management had already invited them back for next year.

Bear gave Sam six orders for BirdBars. Lily had sold out of gardens, but she wanted to keep Charlie's window sill display unit for next year. Charlie received an ass-burning lecture from Jessica, once she found out about Grandpa's Little Helpers. She indicated rather loudly if he ever did that shit again, she'd turn him in herself.

A contrite Charlie said to Bear, Lily and Eunice, "Looks like if I sell next year, it'll have to be Babe Magnets."

Eunice and Charlie went to their rooms early that night, he to sleep and she to plan whatever flight of fancy piqued her interest next. Lily had gone quiet, silently playing Spider Solitaire. She was morose, waiting for Bear to speak up about his plans. But he said not a word.

She hung in there, about to burst. Then he sighed, shut his book on the envelope he was using as a bookmark, and swallowed the last of the cold tea in his cup. These were all Bear signals that he was about to hibernate for the night. As he began to stand, she broke. "For heaven's sake, Bear. You need to tell me. Are you going?"

He looked at her as if he had no idea what was bothering her. "Going to bed? Yep, I'm pooped."

"No, not that, you great pile of oblivious shamus."

Bear looked further confused.

"ARE YOU LEAVING LATIN'S RANCH?"

"What...what are you talking about? Are you ill? Do you need medical attention?"

"When is your family taking you away from us?"

Bear lifted himself from the recliner and swiveled on his cane to the sofa. He plopped down beside her. "Is this what's been eating you tonight?"

"Yes. I need to know. I mean there are plans to make. Who will replace you...how Baby Benny will take it...who'll maintain Sitting Bull..."

"Lily! Stop." He put a paw on her trembling hand but she slapped it away. "I'm glad to discover I have family. Jeff is a good guy. It's nice to know him and his kids."

"And I get that they want you close by. I do. It's good for them and their kids. You'll need new clothes. The Hawaiian shirt is a disaster."

"But Lily, I won't leave Latin's Ranch, not unless Jessica boots my sorry ass to the curb. This is home. This is family. You're all stuck with me. Whatever would make you think I'd do that?"

"For real, Bear?"

"For real, Lily."

Joy swept through her, inside and out. But she certainly couldn't let him see how frightened she had been. She stood with a dramatic yawn. "All right, then. Guess you're stuck with us, too. And the Hawaiian shirt really is a disaster."

CHAPTER FOUR

Case Notes
Nov 20, 10 pm

ACES is over, the gross take counted, the net applied to Latin's Farm maintenance. What a pleasure to present Jessica with a check that is truly from all us residents. She is inclined to add a few chickens to the farm in the spring, since eggs are always in demand for Aurora's kitchen. She's asked Doc to keep his eye open for a farmer with too many cluckers to care for.

Keegan reports that the Iron Man, Alan Medlar, confessed to the murder of Hans Huffman. He's a father furious with anti-vaxxers for exposing his boy to diphtheria, which resulted in permanent heart damage. Diphtheria, of course, is preventable with a vaccine.

His crime of violence is not forgivable but at least understandable. However, there's no excuse for the murder of Cora Stanfield. She was a complete innocent if there ever really is such a thing. In a moment of weakness, Iron Man told Raspy about his son's ordeal. Apparently, he panicked afterwards, knowing he'd said too much. She was sure to put it all together sooner or later, so he shut her up for good. Maybe if she'd called the cops right after their conversation, instead of Alto, there would have been time for her to save herself. Maybe not. Either way, it's up to the courts what to do next.

Although the weather has finally turned to the dour days of November in the Pacific Northwest, this morning brought us a bright bit of good news. Sicilian night will continue as a once a month celebration. We were in doubt on that. Without Frankie to squabble with Aurora over gelato vs fried ice cream, or Mexican vs Italian oregano, well, our cook might be too aggrieved to continue. She loved the old don as much as we did.

Turns out, there was no need to worry. Tonight was the first Sicilian Night without Frankie, and it happened to fall on the Mexican Dìa de Muertos. At breakfast Aurora announced, "We will celebrate the life of our friend. I will prepare his favorites so he celebrates with us. Charlie, I know you use my kitchen when my back is turned." She muttered what might have been a Spanish oath, but I didn't quite get it.

Charlie did. He blanched. "Oh crap."

"So you will replace Frankie as my assistant for this celebration. Come along."

It was a noisy day in the kitchen, Aurora banging pans and squawking at Charlie the same way she did at Frankie. Eventually, we could hear Charlie snarl back at her. Based on the din, we wouldn't be surprised if the old don was out there giving him pointers from on high.

Guests were invited. This time it was Sylvia, Vinny, Tony and Enzo, all here to join the celebration of Frankie. Our spirits lifted as the wine and pasta were passed in his honor. He'll always be one of us.

Conversation flitted around the table, covering the tour of Sicily, who would claim Frankie's private room at Latin's Ranch, and where the new don, his bodyguard and Sylvia would live. Tony, always a handsome man, looked wonderful. Maybe he's grown a wee bit in stature or has a dash more wisdom in his eyes. But that's probably me imagining things. What wasn't imagined was the pleasure in Vinny's face when he looked from his bride to me, his mother-in-law.

In fact, everyone looked happy tonight. I love this eccentric, eclectic clan we've assembled. Our pasts are longer than our futures can ever be, but that doesn't mean we need to live in sorrow for things lost. You build a home from the materials you have on hand. During a lull in the conversation, I leaned to whisper to Bear, "Thank you for staying." He gave me an ursine-sized, cheek-stretching, teeth-revealing smile.

Eventually, the subject of the craft fair came up once again.

"You know," Eunice exclaimed, "while you gumshoes were off busting hooligan heads, I was charming the author selling her books in the booth next to ours. I told her all about Latin's Ranch."

"Busting hooligan heads? Did you bust any hooligan heads, Lily? I didn't bust any hooligan heads."

Eunice ignored Bear and chattered on. "We certainly have a tale or two to tell. Imagine how fun it would be if somebody wrote our stories down. Let people know what a bunch of determined seniors can do. Sure, we need the help of our beloved Jessica to get through our days. But just think about it! We've solved murders, planned weddings, saved crime victims, thwarted a sex offender, healed wounds. Now we're starting a business to help domestic animals. We're really something."

"My cases would be of great interest to nearly anybody," Bear said. We all looked to see if he was being snide. But no, by golly. He actually seemed intrigued. "Some good stuff there."

"My case notes practically tell each story already," I said as a reminder of what I've already composed.

"My exploits would make for steamy reading," said Charlie, wiggling his brows.

Aurora, bringing in a replenished platter of veggies spiked with poblano peppers, declared, "My recipes in a cookbook? Magnífico!"

Sylvia joined in. "I'd love to design a book, cover to cover. Choose the color scheme, the typeface, the paper stock."

Eunice crossed her arms over her Bedazzled chest. "Well then. I think we have our next project. A book about us."

"Maybe a series," I added. Why the hell not? This is exciting.

"'Course, there'd be things we might not want to tell," Charlie said, always the worrier.

"You mean like the fact that you're a womanizing knucklehead?" Bear asked.

"Well, that," answered Charlie. "Or that you're a pontificating crapper with..."

"Gentlemen, please," I said, knowing they'd spar but were friends 'til the end.

"Could be fun," Jessica said, sounding captivated. "I have some horse stories that are very funny. And the project might keep you guys out of...I mean, involved and interested."

She was always looking for ways to keep us out of trouble. She really shouldn't bother. Because if trouble is around, Bear will find it.

And I'll be right here to help.

> *Lily Gilbert, Fulfilled Assistant to PI Bear Jacobs*

AUTHOR'S NOTE:
First Appearances

The three short mystery cases in this book cover a June-November time span in the life of PI Bear Jacobs and the rest of the residents at Latin's Ranch Adult Care Home. Each of the three stories references happenings from the books that have come before:

Fun House Chronicles is a prequel to the mystery series. It explains how most of the characters meet before they move to Latin's Ranch. It also introduces the predator who attacks an elderly woman; he reappears in *Bear and the Burrito*.

Bear in Mind, the first of the mystery series, sets the scene for Lily as an assistant to the retired private investigator, Bear Jacobs. Her case notes are in all three of the short stories. *Bear in Mind* also introduces the geriatric mob boss, Frankie, his bodyguard, Vinnie, and the idea that aide Chrissie is a sure shot, important in *A Bearable Exit*.

Hard to Bear, second in the series, contains the story of two girls who hide in the trailer owned by Sam Hart.

Frankie holes up there with Enzo in *A Bearable Exit*. It is also the source of the red-headed waitress and the moving story of Jo Keegan's failed partnership, both referenced in *Bear and the Burrito*.

Bear Claus, a holiday novella, tells the tale of Sami Bowles who reappears to worry about Charlie in *A Bearable Exit*.

Bear at Sea, third novel in the mystery series, introduces Jo Keegan's new partner who returns in *Clan of the Craft Bear*. It describes the disappearance of the aides mentioned in *Bear and the Burrito,* and introduces the Alaskan Husky, Good Fella, who appears in all three short stories.

ACKNOWLEDGMENTS

Before I get to real people, I'd like to say a bit about the imaginary ones. When I completed *Fun House Chronicles*, the book that introduces this feisty, quirky geriatric gang, I thought I was finished with them. But they weren't finished with me. Much to my surprise, I now have voices in my head. If I ignore the gang too long, writing stories without them, Bear begins to gripe at me. Lily tries to reason. Eunice orders me to get busy. And Charlie pleads to have a successful love life one of these days. They are quite real to me. If some TV producer were to decide a program should be developed, I'd make myself crazy thinking who'd play Bear and Lily.

Now to the real characters who hold pieces of my heart. My take-no-prisoners critique group, Heidi Hansen, Jill Sikes, Melee McGuire. Plus the two members on temporary leave, Jon Eekhoff and Kimberly Minard. Everything I write is better because of them. And I don't think I'd write at all if my sister, Donna Lee Whichello, wasn't here to cheerlead, proofread, and edit.

Finally, a word about the Olympic Peninsula in Washington State, the place where I live. There are so many fine writers out here, maybe because it is nearly impossible to walk these beautiful mountains, woods and trails without having creative thoughts burst free along the way. I doff my verbal hat to you all.

BOOKS BY LINDA B. MYERS

Fun House Chronicles

Self-reliant Lily Gilbert enters a nursing home ready to kick administrative butt until the chill realities of the place nearly flatten her. She calls it the Fun House for the scary sights and sounds that await her there. Soon other quirky residents and caregivers draw Lily and her daughter in as they grapple with their own challenges. Lily discovers each stage of life offers more than a few surprises along the way.

The Bear Jacobs Mystery Series

The characters make their first appearance in *Fun House Chronicles*. Retired PI Bear Jacobs, his eWatson Lily Gilbert, and the rest of the quirky residents are now at Latin's Ranch Adult Family Home in the Pacific Northwest. Yes, they are infirm. Yes, they gripe. But all the while, they solve crimes, dodge bullets and stand tall on their canes, walkers and wheels.

Book One. *Bear in Mind*

The Latin's Ranch residents investigate the case of Charlie's missing wife. Is she a heart breaking bitch who abandoned her hubby? Or is a madman attacking older women? When others in the community disappear, Bear and his gang follow a hazardous and twisted trail to a surprising conclusion.

Book Two. *Hard to Bear*

A vicious crew is producing old-fashioned snuff films with a violent new twist: custom-order murders. The Latin's Ranch gang takes on this updated evil, placing themselves in danger. Bear joins forces with an avenging mob family, a special forces soldier tormented by PTSD, and a pack of mad dogs on the loose in the Pacific Northwest woods.

Novella One. *Bear Claus*

PI Bear Jacobs is mired down with seasonal depression until Lily finds him a mystery to solve. The trail is both fun and fearsome as it leads from theft in the My Fair Pair lingerie shop through a local casino to a perilous solution in the Northwest Forest. *Bear Claus* is a Christmas novella.

Book Three. *Bear at Sea*

When Eunice wins the Arctic Angel Award, the Latin's Ranch gang cruises to Alaska to pick up her prize. But high life on shipboard is dashed by low life murderers and thieves. One of their aides is struck down, and Eunice's life is threatened not once but twice. The gang takes action, endangering themselves to solve the case of the short-tailed albatross.

Book Four. *Three Bears*

Three short mystery cases in one book. *Bear and the Burrito* marks the return of a dangerous predator; *A Bearable Exit* has the don Frankie turning over the mob reins to his grandson but only if Lily's daughter accepts a unique proposal; *Clan of the Craft Bear* tackles the murder of a woodworker by electrocution and introduces a nephew who could take Bear away from Latin's Ranch.

Secrets of the Big Island

Life is uncomplicated in a Big Island village until Maile Palea, an 8-year-old girl, disappears. Twelve years later she is still missing. Her sister and brother never give up trying to find her and cannot heal until they do; a village no longer feels safe from a changing world; a perpetrator discovers what disastrous things happen when you keep secrets too long. A perfect read for fans of edgy suspense and hot Hawaiian nights.

Creation of Madness

Oregon, 1989. Psychologist Laura Covington joins a community mental health department. One of her new clients suffers Multiple Personality Disorder. Through him, Laura discovers a desert cult and the vicious psychopath who practices mind control on children. Laura has unleashed dangerous secrets, and now, she must decide how far she is willing to go to protect everything she loves. WARNING: This is psychological suspense that borders on horror...it's geared to keep you guessing as it builds toward its unpredictable conclusion.

The Slightly Altered History of Cascadia

The gods have screwed up the creation of humans. They create a humanoid spirit, Cascadia, to fix up what they've screwed up. To prepare for life among humans, Cascadia learns the use of lust by Helen of Troy, the art of the knife by Jim Bowie, and more skills from other gods and historical humans. Along with the help of her human familiar, a magic blade, a flying bear, and a logging horse named Blue, Cascadia rids the woods of many evils. This fantasy for grown-ups is part magical reality, part myths, and all fun.

Fog Coast Runaway

Adelia Wright never knew her mother. Her father, a lighthouse keeper far out to sea, is distant, literally and figuratively. After her brother terrorizes her, Adelia runs away into the wilds of the 1890s Oregon Coast. Her perilous journey takes her to Seaside, where she works in the scullery of a posh hotel. She is soon on the run again, sought regarding a murdered guest...this time with a frightened little boy in tow. Adelia shelters in a logging camp, then moves on to Swilltown in what is today's Astoria. Her path includes abandonment and romance, sorrow and joy. This is historical fiction for anyone who loves the pioneer spirit and the wilds of the Pacific Northwest.

ABOUT THE AUTHOR

Linda B. Myers won her first creative contest in the sixth grade. After a Chicago marketing career, she traded in snow boots for rain boots and moved to the Pacific Northwest with her Maltese, Dotty. You can visit with Linda at facebook.com/lindabmyers.author or email her at myerslindab@gmail.com.

Made in the
USA
Middletown, DE